Ivy thought of Jackson's peachy complexion –
if he was human and put on that spray tan, he'd
look like an orange. But he looked completely
normal. Completely human. Which meant that
without fake tan his skin must be really,
really pale. Could Jackson be . . .
'A vampire,' Ivy whispered.

Sink your fangs into these:

🦇

Switched

Fangtastic!

Revamped!

Vampalicious

🦇

Coming soon:

Love Bites

Sienna Mercer

MY SISTER THE VAMPIRE

TAKE TWO

EGMONT

With special thanks to Sara O'Connor

For Neil. This time every page is yours.

EGMONT
We bring stories to life

My Sister the Vampire: Take Two first published in Great Britain 2011
by Egmont UK Limited
239 Kensington High Street
London W8 6SA

Copyright © Working Partners Ltd 2011
Created by Working Partners Limited, London WC1X 9HH

ISBN 978 1 4052 5697 1

3 5 7 9 10 8 6 4 2

A CIP catalogue record for this title is available from the British Library

Typeset by Avon DataSet Ltd, Bidford on Avon, Warwickshire
Printed and bound in Great Britain by the CPI Group

Chapter One

Ivy Vega was trapped inside her worst night-mare.

'Welcome to Mister Smoothie. I'll be your elixir mixer.' The girl's smile was almost as big as the one on the store's cartoon logo. 'What can I fix for you lovely people today?'

Too. Much. Perky. Ivy wanted to shade her eyes.

'I . . . well . . . um . . .' Ivy's dad stared at the huge pink menu behind the girl's head.

'We just need a minute.' Ivy pulled him to one side to let a little girl in plaits and her mom go in front of them.

'I design skyscrapers,' he muttered, running his hand through his usually neat black hair. 'I should be able to order a smoothie like a regular person.'

'You're about two hundred years away from *regular*, Dad,' Ivy whispered, glancing over her shoulder to make sure no one behind them could overhear.

Just this morning, Mr Vega had announced that he wanted to take his two daughters out. Ivy had tried to go to an establishment more suited to his tastes, but he'd insisted that he should get to know Olivia in the world she was used to – which meant the bunniest place in town.

'It says here to pick a size and a special flavour.' Ivy handed him a menu. 'Or you can make your own from the list.'

He opened the complicated menu, turning it over to look at all the choices. 'Do apples and carrots really go together?'

'I've had that once before.' Ivy nodded, her plastic bat earrings bouncing. 'It's an odd combination, but it works.'

He smiled. 'Just like my beautiful twin daughters.'

Ivy looked across the restaurant to where her sister, Olivia Abbott, was waiting in the farthest booth, watching them. She knew this wasn't one of the vampire-friendly restaurants in town and she looked worried for them. *Perhaps Olivia should be up here ordering*, Ivy thought. In her pink knit sweater and designer jeans, she fitted in here much more than Ivy and her dad, both in black from head to toe.

'Are you ready?' the server girl asked pointedly. It looked like her happiness was as fake as the tropical flowers hanging from the ceiling.

'How about I go first?' Ivy volunteered. She scanned the list of fruity concoctions. Crushed

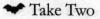

Blushed was too perky for her and Beauty-Boosting Blueberry was too silly. Ivy needed something with a little bite. Ah ha! She caught the eye of the server and asked, 'Could I please have a Red Lipsmacker?'

'Is that a Mini-Mummy, Midi-Dum-Di-Dum or Mega-Mighty?'

Ivy struggled not to roll her eyes. 'Small, please. Oh – and no ice.'

The girl grabbed a cup, scribbled on it and shouted, 'One Mini-Mum Smacker – no crunch.'

Ivy glanced at her dad and saw him opening and closing his mouth like a goldfish. The mini/midi/mega options were clearly too much for him to process. 'Let's get this over with,' he muttered. He took a deep breath and slapped the menu down on the counter. 'I'm going to have a Midi-Dum-Di-Dum Twist and Shout. Please. And for my daughter –'

'A Twist and Shout?' the serving girl interrupted. 'Are you sure?'

'Yes, I am.' Mr Vega nodded.

Ivy had a feeling something bad was about to happen.

'You don't want more time to make up your mind?' She pressed the menu back into his hand.

'No . . . no,' Mr Vega was insistent, firmly handing the menu back. 'That's the smoothie I've chosen and that's the smoothie I want. A Twist and Shout for me.'

What's wrong with a Twist and Shout? Ivy wondered. *Is it really difficult to make?* The menu just said crushed ice with an orange and cranberry swirl; sounded simple enough.

The girl sighed. 'All right.' Then she took a deep breath and called out, 'Hey, Mister Smoothie!'

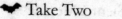

Mr Vega's face dropped as the entire store shouted back, 'Hey, what?'

Ivy shot a panicked look at her sister, who was cringing.

The girl called, 'I've got a little twist!' Understanding the routine, all the regular customers replied, 'I've got a little SHOUT!' Then someone hit the jukebox and the five teenage employees, including the girl who had served them, jumped up on the counter, twisting to the song as it blasted out of every speaker. An old couple in the corner stood up and started wiggling their hips, too.

Mr Vega looked utterly mortified, his face pale . . . r than usual. He gripped the counter as though to stop himself from fleeing the scene. Ivy would have been right behind him.

I will never set foot in here again, Ivy vowed as everyone danced around her.

The serving girl even grabbed her dad's hands to get him to dance, so he bobbed his knees a couple of times and tried to smile. Ivy had seen more convincing smiles on corpses.

My worst nightmare just got worse, Ivy thought. *Now Dad's dancing.*

After an eternity, the Midi-Dum-Di-Dum Twist and Shout was plonked down on the counter.

'Is there anything else?' the serving girl asked, slightly breathless.

'Um,' Mr Vega clutched the crumpled menu. 'If I say "Pinkaholic" will there be any more . . . er . . . performances?'

'No, sir,' the girl said, 'the Pinkaholic has nothing special except the taste. Should I go ahead and get you that?'

'Yes, please,' Mr Vega said, sighing with relief.

The girl leaned forward and whispered to him, 'You see the little musical notes on the menu?

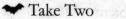

You might want to sidestep those smoothies when you come back next time.'

'Next time?' asked Ivy's dad with alarm. 'Yes . . . next time.'

When the smoothie arrived, her dad paid, picked up the bright pink and yellow cups and stepped tight-lipped over to the table where Olivia was waiting. Ivy could see his hands shaking.

'I should have warned you,' Olivia said, trying to keep the smile off her face as her dad placed her drink down on the bright orange table. 'There are a few smoothies to avoid if you aren't into spontaneous group singing.'

'Hmm,' Mr Vega replied, sliding into the booth across from the twins. 'I'm all for trying new things, but spontaneous group singing isn't one of them.'

'Thank the darkness,' Ivy breathed.

Olivia was really happy her biological dad was going out of his way to get to know her. He already knew a lot about Ivy – she lived with him, after all. It was only a couple of weeks ago, just before Christmas, when Olivia found out he was her and Ivy's real dad.

She took a big slurp of her smoothie and then started coughing and spluttering. She tried to compose herself but Mr Vega had already noticed.

His face fell. 'Is that not . . . did I get it wrong?'

Should I tell him? Olivia wondered. She didn't want to hurt his feelings, but at the same time, she didn't want to have to force down the whole mushy, sticky drink. 'I'm not a big fan of bananas,' Olivia confessed.

Mr Vega groaned. 'I apologise, Olivia. How about we switch?'

Olivia nodded, gratefully. The Twist and Shout

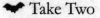

was one of her favourites – especially because of the dancing.

'This simply demonstrates my point,' Mr Vega went on, 'that I must spend more time getting to know you. Which I intend to do as soon as I get back.'

Ivy looked up from her drink. 'Get back from where?'

'Another reason I wanted to see you both together is to say that, since we are no longer moving to Europe –'

'Woohoo!' Ivy and Olivia said in unison. Just last week, the twins had been forced to try every trick in the book to avert disaster and convince Mr Vega not to leave Franklin Grove.

'There are some urgent things I must take care of,' he continued. 'I have already spoken with your mother, Olivia.' He was talking about Mrs Abbott, her adopted mom. Neither of the girls could remember their biological mother. 'She has agreed to let Ivy stay with you for the next few nights.'

Olivia looked at her twin. 'Sleepover!' she squealed, causing the couple in the next booth to stare at them.

Ivy grinned. The smoothie had turned her teeth red. 'I've been wanting to repaint my nails.' Ivy held up her hand to reveal chipped silver nail polish. 'But what's the trip, Dad?'

Mr Vega waved a hand dismissively, revealing his cuff link shaped like a miniature coffin. 'It is just some business I must attend to without delay.'

'Where are you going?' Olivia persisted. *We've barely had one smoothie together and already he's leaving!* she thought.

'Uh, Dallas has a lot of new construction going on,' Mr Vega said. 'Anyway, I won't be gone more than a couple of days and I will be back before school starts. Now, let's talk about something more interesting.'

'Like the presents you're going to bring back for us?' Ivy said.

'Like what that Lipsmacker tastes like,' Mr Vega said to Ivy, making a grab for her cup. 'Let's switch.'

They swapped around their smoothies and slurped. Olivia had a hundred questions she wanted to ask her bio-dad about his family and where she and Ivy came from – but for now she was just happy that they were together without any more secrets.

They traded smoothies again so that Ivy could try the Twist and Shout but then got confused about which smoothie was which.

'At least I'd never get the two of you mixed up,' Mr Vega said.

Olivia kept a straight face and didn't look at

her sister. *So maybe there's one tiny secret he doesn't know*, Olivia thought. She and Ivy had switched lots of times to fool Mr Vega and everyone else, too. She felt Ivy squeeze her hand under the table.

Olivia noticed the mini-jukebox sitting on the table next to the box of napkins. 'Ooh, let's pick a song!'

Mr Vega paled. 'As long as there is no audience participation.'

She giggled. 'We'll be careful.' She turned the old-fashioned knob to flip through the list of songs that came up on a screen. 'How about "The Right One"?' Olivia stopped on the theme tune from the new rom com she'd dragged Ivy to see two days ago.

'Ugh, I'm so sick of that song,' Ivy said. 'And it's only your favourite movie because you have a crush on Jackson Caulfield.'

'I do not!' Olivia tried to stop herself blushing. 'OK, maybe I do – but we don't have to talk about that now.' She didn't want her bio-dad to think she was boy-crazy. She flicked through the song list in an attempt to change the subject.

'Wait!' Mr Vega cried out, making her jump. 'You passed the perfect song.' He took over the knob and twisted until it came back to 'Double Trouble'.

'I love that one!' Olivia hummed the tune and tapped her feet.

As the catchy song played out over the speakers, he pulled his straw in and out of the smoothie cup, making a little squeaking noise. 'Now that I know your favourite movie,' he said thoughtfully, 'how about your favourite book?'

Olivia felt silly admitting it in front of her vampire family. 'I really love the Count Vira vampire books.'

Mr Vega gave a dashing smile. 'You might be surprised to learn that I have a first-edition signed copy of *Love in the Black of Night* in my library.'

Ivy's jaw dropped and Olivia squealed.

'Oh my goodness, you have to show it to me!' That was the first Count Vira book she had ever read.

'I promise I will.' Mr Vega kept squeaking his straw in between sips. 'How about your favourite subject in school?'

'I love art class,' Olivia said.

'*Art*? Is that so?' he replied. 'You know I –'

Ivy's phone blasted out the first riffs of the *Phantom of the Opera* musical, interrupting them.

'Sorry,' Ivy mouthed as she answered the call. 'Hey . . . Yeah . . . OK . . .' From her smile, Olivia could tell Ivy was talking to her boyfriend, Brendan. Whenever she was around him, Ivy's usual goth grouch turned into adorable goth glee.

While Ivy chatted, Olivia took a moment to study Mr Vega's face. With his strong jaw and dark eyebrows, he looked like he belonged on the cover of Count Vira's books.

'You know, Olivia, I'm an art enthusiast,' Mr Vega said. 'I would dearly love to see some of your work.'

Olivia beamed. 'OK!'

Even though her bio-dad's style was on the opposite end of the colour spectrum, he had excellent taste. He was even setting up a new exhibit at the Franklin Grove museum.

'Brendan wants to have lunch at the Meat & Greet later,' Ivy explained, putting her phone in her bag.

'Just you two?' Olivia asked.

'Everybody. He's already texted Sophia and Camilla.'

'What a thoughtful young man,' Mr Vega said.

'Do you have a sweetheart, Olivia?'

For the past few months, what with settling into her new home and discovering her new family in Franklin Grove, Olivia hadn't had a moment to think about romance.

'Nope,' Olivia said. 'I never have had. But seeing Brendan and Ivy together makes me wish I did.'

Ivy smiled her shy little smile. Olivia knew her sister had crushed on Brendan for years but hadn't spoken a word to him until Olivia accidentally broke the ice during a twin switch.

Mr Vega stopped squeaking the straw. 'Do you mean . . . Do you want someone *like* Brendan?'

'Oh, no.' Olivia could see what he was getting at. He fell in love with her human mother and that made his life totally complicated. 'I'm looking for a perfectly normal boy – without any, erm, unusual eating habits.'

Mr Vega started squeaking the straw again. 'I see. Well, I am certain that the perfect someone for you would have to be a very special kind of normal.'

'I second that,' Ivy said, bumping her shoulder into Olivia's.

I'm so lucky to have a new dad and new sister, thought Olivia.

'Now, I spotted some chocolate-chip cookies on the menu,' Mr Vega said, slurping the last bit of his drink noisily. 'I'll ask the waitress to bring three over.' He raised a hand in the air.

'There aren't any waitresses,' Olivia said. 'You'll have to go back up to the counter.'

'Oh.' Mr Vega looked like he would rather gulp down a garlic smoothie. But he eased himself out of the booth and went to stand back in line.

Ivy and Olivia grinned at each other.

'He must really want to spend time with me to

risk another sing along,' Olivia commented.

'No kidding,' Ivy agreed, as she watched Mr Vega chatting to the server. 'He's the best real dad we could have.'

🦇   🦇   🦇

An hour later, the twins were walking to the Meat & Greet with their friends. It was cold so Olivia had wrapped herself up in her matching pink scarf and gloves set.

'How was your morning?' Camilla Edmunson asked.

'Let's just say it was pretty . . . musical,' Olivia answered, smiling at the memory of Mr Vega dancing.

'My head almost imploded when Olivia wanted to put on "The Right One",' Ivy said to Brendan, sticking out her tongue and pretending to strangle herself.

'I love that song!' Camilla declared at the same

time as Sophia Hewitt said, 'Torture!'

Olivia was on one side of Ivy and Brendan, and Camilla was on the other. They started singing 'The Right One' as loud as they could, forming a surround sound of chipper elevator music.

'Nooo,' Ivy screeched, covering her ears with her woolly black mittens. 'I'm melting!'

Olivia wasn't about to stop now. She gave Camilla a wink and the two of them started dancing around Ivy and Brendan, still singing the cheesy lyrics: 'You're the right one for me, can't you seeeeee?'

Sophia removed the lens cap from her camera and snapped a few shots. 'Ivy, you look like Frosty the Snowman at an ice-carving contest.'

Ivy was wearing an ankle-length mauve jacket with big black buttons down the front and had her eyes shut trying to block out the dancing.

Everyone laughed.

'It's safe to come out now, Ivy,' Brendan teased. 'The happy people have stopped singing.'

Everyone laughed harder.

'Enough!' Ivy cried. 'We have an evil alert at twenty paces.' She was looking down the street at three girls walking towards them.

It was Charlotte Brown and two hangers on. Her blonde hair was poking out from under her white fluffy hat. Olivia wasn't Charlotte's biggest fan, but they had to cheer together on the squad and so she wanted to avoid any major incident.

Unfortunately, Olivia thought, *something always happens whenever Ivy and Charlotte are within a mile of each other.*

Charlotte stopped and scowled at them until she caught sight of Olivia. She plastered on a big smile. 'Olivia, darling!'

Olivia smiled at her, Katie and Allison, while Ivy and the rest of the group waited a few feet away. Charlotte turned her back on everyone else, making Olivia feel even more awkward.

'We're going to Mister Smoothie to compare Christmas presents,' Charlotte said. 'Come with us.' Katie and Allison nodded like bobble heads in their matching lavender scarves.

'Oh, we've just left there,' Olivia explained.

'*They* were at Mister Smoothie?' Charlotte squinted at Olivia's friends.

Ivy piped up. 'We even got a Twist and Shout.' Ivy began doing a silly version of the dance right there on the sidewalk. Brendan, Sophia and Camilla joined in while Olivia tried not to laugh.

'Haven't you moved yet?' Charlotte snapped at Ivy. 'I can't wait to get some normal neighbours.'

Ivy opened her mouth, no doubt with a cutting come-back, but Brendan beat her to it.

'Good news,' Brendan replied smoothly. 'Ivy's not going to Europe.'

'Did they refuse to let you in for crimes against fashion?' Charlotte smirked. Katie and Allison giggled.

'It turns out I'm needed here,' Ivy retorted, 'for a campaign against conformity.'

Charlotte blinked. Olivia could tell she didn't really understand the insult. *Which is a good thing*, Olivia thought.

'Whatever,' Charlotte huffed.

Olivia jumped in. 'Is that a new bag, Charlotte?'

Charlotte shifted the big, brown, expensive-looking bag on her shoulder. 'It's a Kevin Green. My daddy bought it for me in New York.'

'It's nice,' said Olivia, not quite sure if the over-sized leather bag went with Charlotte's shiny blue puffy jacket.

'Did you say Kevin Greene?' Brendan peered closer at the bag. Olivia couldn't imagine Brendan having an interest in handbag designers.

'Yes,' said Charlotte, turning her nose up at having to reply to Brendan.

'I think your logo is supposed to have an extra "e" on the end of Green.' Brendan straightened up and put his arm around Ivy.

'What!' Charlotte spluttered and Katie and Allison gathered around for a closer look.

Katie's horrified gasp was all Olivia needed to realise that Charlotte's bag was a cheap knock off. Charlotte stomped away, her friends scurrying after her. 'At least I won't be mistaken for a zombie,' she called back over her shoulder.

Ivy laughed and gave Brendan a huge hug. 'That was killer.'

'Impressive fashion knowledge, Brendan,' Olivia said. 'How did you know about the "e"?'

Brendan shrugged. 'Little sisters have their uses. Bethany's been educating me on a weekly basis about who is wearing what.'

Sophia waved her camera, her white smile lighting up her dark skin. 'I got it! The very moment when Charlotte saw for herself.'

'You devil,' Ivy said, making Sophia show her on the camera's little screen.

'Come on, guys,' said Brendan, 'I'm hungry!'

'Onward to the Meat & Greet!' said Camilla in her captain-of-the-space-ship voice.

'Onward!' everyone responded.

As they walked, they talked about the presents they'd gotten from their family – no one else was lucky enough to get an elusive Kevin Greene, but Olivia loved the pink, sparkly earmuffs her parents had bought her that matched her old scarf and glove set. They were keeping her ears toasty warm in the cold.

'What did you get Ivy, Brendan?' Camilla asked.

Brendan and Ivy shared a look.

Ivy explained, 'He gave me a season ticket to

the movie theatre, a year-long subscription to *Vamp!* magazine and a bus pass.'

Olivia realised that everything Brendan had given Ivy were things that needed a permanent address in Franklin Grove. 'How romantic!'

'There isn't anything romantic about a bus pass,' Sophia declared.

'Yes, there is,' Ivy and Brendan said quietly to each other.

'Cheese!' Sophia complained. 'This registers cheese factor 10!'

Ivy just smiled and Olivia wished for the second time that day that she'd be as lucky in love.

'I've never heard of *Vamp!* magazine,' Camilla said as they came to the end of the street. Camilla didn't have any idea about the vampires in Franklin Grove, and it had to stay that way.

'Oh, we're almost there!' Olivia chirped,

changing the subject quickly.

'And I can't wait for a ketchup-smothered chunky burger,' Brendan declared. 'With fries.'

But as they turned the corner to the diner, Ivy suddenly threw her arms out. *'What is that?'*

Olivia couldn't see anything unusual. The diner had the same piñatas and disco balls hanging from meat hooks in the windows, the same sandwich board outside boasting the best burgers in town. 'Um . . . it's the Meat & Greet?'

'No,' Ivy said, frowning her forehead into a V. 'It's not. Look!' She pointed to the sign above the door.

Sophia and Brendan gasped. Then, Olivia realised that not only was the restaurant completely empty, the neon sign no longer read 'Meat & Greet'. It was 'Meet & Greet' with two 'e's!

'What is it with "e"s today?' Brendan asked.

'What does it mean?' Ivy said, clearly worried.

This could mean trouble, Olivia thought. Had it become a regular diner? If it had, where would the vamps eat out now? Or had someone exposed their secret?

Camilla jumped up and down, her blonde curls bouncing. 'I know! We've entered an alternate universe; the aliens who created it have obviously gotten some things wrong.' Camilla was a huge sci-fi fan.

Olivia couldn't decide which was worse: an alien invasion or the existence of vampires being exposed. She was one of the few humans who knew the big secret and had taken a vow never to break the Laws of the Night, the very first being: Don't Tell Anyone About Vampires EVER!

Ivy started walking faster towards the diner,

with everyone hurrying to keep up.

Ivy stopped at the diner's door to read a sign explaining that the Meat & Greet – with the 'a' – would be closed for a week.

'Phew,' Ivy said. 'I was about to stake somebody.'

Camilla was still suspicious. 'But why is the sign different?'

A rumbling noise filled the air. The five friends listened, huddled on the step in front of the diner's door. The cold wind picked up and whipped Olivia's hair in front of her face. It was the noise of an engine, a great big engine – or maybe lots of engines.

A convoy of trucks trundled down the road towards them. 'Harker Films' was emblazoned on each one.

'It's not aliens,' said Camilla, clearly disappointed.

'No,' Sophia replied, her eyes shining as the

trucks turned into the diner's parking lot. 'It's Hollywood!' She rubbed her hands with glee.

'The Meat & Greet must be a movie set. This completely sucks!' Olivia said, using the vampire phrase for all things awesome.

'But what about my burger?' Brendan said.

Ivy gave him a sympathetic hug as the trucks formed a large rectangle around the parking lot. There was a clatter of metal against concrete as burly men in thick sweaters banged down ramps from the back of the trucks and hauled out trolleys of speakers, enormous lights and costume racks.

A pair of men started putting up a line of plastic building barriers along the sidewalk.

'Franklin Grove?' said one with a few holes in his sweater. 'Whoever heard of this place?'

'Not me,' muttered his companion. 'They don't even have a coffee shop.'

'I hope Hollywood isn't going to be as snobby as Charlotte Brown,' Ivy said.

Finally, a group of long trailers arrived. From the size of them and the gold stars on the doors, Olivia guessed they were the private dressing rooms for the actors. Passers-by were starting to take notice and come over to see what was happening.

'I can't wait to find out what movie it is,' Sophia said.

'And who's starring in it,' Olivia added. She loved following Hollywood gossip. The latest issue of *Celeb Weekly* was always on her bedside table.

As they spoke, a huge bald man in sunglasses with bulging arms approached them. He was wearing an ear piece and his jacket had the Harker Films logo with a nametag that read 'Jerome'.

'Welcome to Franklin Grove,' Olivia said brightly.

This seemed to startle him and he lowered his sunglasses to get a good look at them. 'Thank you,' he said in a deep voice. 'But I'm afraid I'm going to have to ask you to vacate the premises.'

'Yes, sir,' Camilla squeaked, looking like Goldilocks facing off with the biggest bear.

'Before we go, would you please tell us what the movie is?' Olivia asked.

'Technically, I'm not allowed,' Jerome said. 'But since you're so polite, I can let you in on a little secret: if you wait just behind that third barrier from the end, the star will be arriving in about five minutes.'

Olivia beamed. 'Ooh, thanks!'

Jerome gave them a wink and then called out to one of the roadies, 'Hey, you! What do you think you're doing with those lights?'

'Being nice always pays off,' Olivia said to Ivy as they moved towards the barriers.

The five friends hurried to a spot at the front of the growing crowd. There were the Meat & Greet waitresses on their day off, hairdressers from the salon across the street and even ladies in curlers trying to see what was happening. Everyone was gossiping about who the movie's lead might be.

Right on time, an SUV with tinted windows pulled up to the barricade as their new friend Jerome shifted one of the waist-high plastic barriers to let it in. Olivia felt the crowd surge forward, pressing her into one of the barriers.

Sophia snapped away with her camera and even Ivy was stretching her neck to catch a glimpse. The back door opened and out came a faded brown cowboy boot, followed by a well-worn pair of jeans and then a trademark flash of white teeth.

Olivia's heart was shaking like a pompom. She

felt her cheeks turn hot and she couldn't move.

'Olivia,' asked Ivy, 'are you OK?'

Olivia had to remind herself to breathe. 'I don't believe it,' she said and grabbed her sister's arm. 'It's him!'

Chapter Two

'Jackson Caulfield!' shrieked a young girl behind Ivy, almost bursting her eardrum.

Not bad, Ivy thought, *for a bunny*. His scruffy blond hair and blue eyes were definitely not Ivy's thing, but she could see why millions of bunnies – including Olivia – would get excited. Jackson smiled and, as he waved at the crowd, his green army jacket flapped open to reveal a rock band T-shirt.

'He's even cuter in real life,' Olivia whispered, not taking her eyes off him.

'Jackson!' the voice behind Ivy screeched

again. 'Can I have your autograph?' The girl, wearing a pink and blue polka-dot jacket, leaned over Ivy's shoulder and waved a slightly crumpled magazine with him on the cover.

Jackson strolled over, with Jerome and another security guard watching closely. 'Sure you can,' he said with a slight southern drawl.

The girl's excited shriek increased in volume with every step that Jackson took towards them, and Ivy could see Olivia had squeezed over to let her come to the barrier.

'What's your name?' Jackson asked, relaxed, as he signed an autograph for her. The girl just shrieked louder and started to cry.

Ivy nudged her sister. 'Why don't you say hello?' she whispered.

'I can't!' Olivia whispered back.

What's going on? Ivy thought. *Olivia never has trouble talking to people!*

Ivy poked Olivia in the side, making her yelp.

Jackson looked right at her and smiled.

'Hi, Jackson,' Camilla said from just behind Olivia.

'Hello,' he said. 'What's your name?'

'I'm Camilla,' she said. 'I loved you in *The Right One.*'

'Thanks,' he replied with an easy grin. 'That was my favourite shoot so far.'

'And I'm Sophia.' Sophia held up her camera. 'Can I take your picture?'

'Sure,' he said and smiled as he posed, producing a mixture of sighs and screams from the crowd behind while Sophia snapped away.

'And who are you?' he asked.

He's singling out Olivia! Ivy thought with excitement.

'Um, hi,' Olivia said, staring down at her faux-fur-lined boots.

'This is Olivia,' Ivy prompted.

Jackson leaned forward a little, so that the whole crowd couldn't hear. 'It was really nice of you to let that girl come through,' he said to Olivia.

Still, Olivia didn't speak. The closest she could get to looking at him was staring at his cowboy boots. 'That's because Olivia *is* really nice,' Ivy replied.

Why isn't she saying anything? Ivy thought. *If she doesn't do it now, she'll regret it for eternity! Maybe longer.*

'Yeehaw,' Olivia blurted out.

Oh my darkness, she's gone mad! Ivy thought. Olivia's pink face told her that she didn't know why in bat's name she had said it either.

'I mean, uh – I like your boots,' Olivia muttered. Her pink cheeks turned bright red.

'Thanks,' he replied, with a chuckle.

Behind him, a power-suited red-headed woman

climbed out of the SUV, yakking into a phone.

'I'm in charge of his image,' she was saying, 'and there will be *no* clown outfit.'

She waved Jackson back to the car.

One of the hairdressers was leaning over the rail, trying to catch Jackson's attention. 'Hey, Jackson!'

But his eyes didn't stray from Olivia. 'That's my manager. I've got to go to work. I'm glad you like my boots.' He smiled. 'I like your fuzzy earmuffs.'

Then Jackson waved goodbye to the crowd and disappeared between the trucks into the parking lot.

'I love you, Jackson!' the polka-dot girl called after him.

Ivy was still thinking about how much attention Jackson had paid to Olivia. 'Well, that was interesting,' she said.

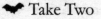

'He's so nice!' declared Sophia.

'And really cute, too,' Camilla added. 'Isn't he, Olivia?'

Olivia covered her face with her hands. 'I just made the most enormous idiot of myself! "*Yeehaw*, I like your boots?" Is that the best I could come up with?'

Brendan chuckled. 'You looked like a tomato with fuzzy pink earmuffs.'

'She did not!' Ivy said. 'She was charming him with her beauty.'

'So much for keeping my cool around celebrities,' Olivia muttered.

'But he's not just any celebrity,' Camilla said. 'He's Jackson Caulfield!'

'That's what makes it worse!' Olivia groaned.

But Ivy didn't think it was so embarrassing. Jackson hadn't been able to keep his eyes off Olivia – that much was obvious. Ivy felt an idea brewing. Maybe Franklin Grove's newest bunny was the right guy for her sister? She was so happy with Brendan. She'd love for Olivia to have the same with someone.

'Can we *please* go get something to eat now?' Brendan asked, interrupting her thoughts.

'Anything to escape more humiliation,' Olivia said.

'How about back to Mister Smoothie?' Camilla suggested.

'I would rather dig my own grave,' Ivy replied. 'Anyway, I've got to get back home before Dad leaves.'

'No burger?' Brendan pouted, looking back at the Meat & Greet longingly.

'Unless you're happy with a movie-version that's all cornstarch and glue, you won't be getting a burger today.' Ivy took Brendan's hand as they started to walk away.

They wove their way through the crowd that was still pressing forward to catch a glimpse of Jackson.

'Excuse me,' Olivia said, squeezing past three little girls jumping up and down.

'Sorry.' Camilla bumped into a skinny pizza-delivery boy, still holding warm pizza boxes.

'Careful!' Sophia said as a woman with her Pekinese dog knocked her camera.

Ivy took control. In her loudest voice she said to Olivia, 'What do you mean you don't like Jackson Caulfield?'

The crowd gasped and parted – almost afraid to be infected by anti-Jackson sentiment.

'You think he's a bad actor?' Ivy called out and their path got even wider. Olivia had her face in her hands. 'Ivy!' she whispered with gritted teeth.

'We're getting through, aren't we?' Ivy whispered.

'Phew,' Brendan said as they finally escaped.

When they turned the corner, they ran into Charlotte and her minions coming back with smoothies in their hands. All three cheerleaders had slightly blue-stained lips. Ivy realised that they must have all gone for the Beauty-Boosting Blueberry. Charlotte had turned her bag around, so no one could read the logo.

'People were saying something was happening at the Meat & Greet.' Charlotte prompted Olivia for information, but Ivy wasn't about to let the chance go by.

'Oh yes.' Ivy forced a look of concern on to her face. 'There must have been dozens of men there – and the smell was awful!'

Charlotte crinkled her nose. 'Smell?'

Brendan caught on quickly. 'A pipe could have burst or maybe something happened to the sewers?'

'I'd avoid the whole area if I were you,' Ivy said. *Little Miss Superior will just have to wait to see the hottest actor in Hollywood*, she thought. Charlotte would find out sooner or later.

Charlotte considered for a second and then said, 'I wanted go to the mall, anyway.'

'We can look at bags,' Katie suggested, getting a sharp look from Charlotte.

As the three girls walked away, Olivia wagged her finger at Ivy. 'Naughty, naughty.'

'I know,' Ivy said, feeling a pleasant tingle at her own wickedness.

Their dad was rolling a small suitcase across the porch when Ivy and Olivia arrived at the top of Undertaker Hill. He looked a little broody in his smart jacket and crisp white collared shirt, but as soon as he saw the girls, his face creased in a smile.

He wheeled the suitcase over to the car. 'Perfect timing! I was going to wait until you came back, but since you're here, I might be able to catch an earlier flight. Have you had a fun afternoon?'

'Olivia met the love of her life,' Ivy said.

'No, I did not!' Olivia voice had gone up an octave. She cleared her throat. 'He's just an actor I admire.' She had been trying to push that humiliating performance out of her mind. 'And I'm sure he thinks I'm a total idiot.'

Mr Vega raised an eyebrow. 'Impossible.'

Like Ivy said, Olivia thought, *the best real dad I could wish for.*

'But a movie star doesn't sound like a normal boyfriend to me,' Mr Vega said.

'Very true,' Olivia replied. *It doesn't matter anyway*, she thought. *Tomato-with-earmuffs or not, I'd never have a chance with him.*

'Now, girls,' Mr Vega said. 'Audrey will be over to pick you up in two hours and, when I come back, I hope we can spend much more time together as a family.' He planted a kiss on Ivy's forehead, then held his arm out for Olivia to join them in a group hug. Every hug from her bio-dad felt like ten hugs, like he was trying to make up for the time they'd spent apart.

'Just not at Mister Smoothie.' Mr Vega grinned as he got into the car.

Olivia giggled. As her bio-dad drove away, Olivia said to Ivy, 'We really are a family now, aren't we?'

Ivy nodded. 'And I can't imagine life any different. So will you come in and help me finish packing my stuff for the sleepover?' she asked.

Olivia took one look at the innocent smile on her sister's face. She mustered up her best imitation of one of Ivy's trademark death stares.

'You must think I was born yesterday,' she said, folding her arms.

Ivy burst out laughing. 'OK, OK. Will you help me *start* packing?'

Chapter Three

Olivia's mom was very excited indeed when they got home. 'I love sleepovers!' she declared. 'Olivia hasn't had one since we moved here.'

Olivia helped Ivy haul her heavy black duffel bag down the hall and dumped it at the bottom of the stairs. There had been lots of debate over how many pairs of boots Ivy should bring (two), how many chunky sweaters (three) and, of course, which nail polish colours (Goddess of the Night, Diva at Dusk and Vampy Violet).

'Thank you for having me, Audrey,' Ivy said.

'We're thrilled you're staying over,' Olivia's dad said, poking his head out of the living room. 'I greet the sun with an hour of tai chi every morning. Beginners welcome, if you're awake.'

Olivia rolled her eyes. Her dad was always a little too inclusive with his martial-arts hobby, but Ivy was nodding along like she planned to join him.

Mrs Abbott clapped her hands together. 'Steve, will you take Ivy's bag up to Olivia's room?'

'Ah,' said Mr Abbott, after only one lift of the duffel. 'A worthy opponent. A moment's meditation is needed before attempting to move this mountain.' He closed his eyes and took several deep breaths.

Olivia giggled.

'I hope you're hungry,' said Mrs Abbott.

Olivia felt her tummy rumble. With all the excitement of the movie people showing up and

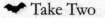

then working her way through Ivy's enormous and scattered wardrobe, she'd barely eaten all afternoon.

'I'm starving,' Ivy said.

Mrs Abbott ushered the girls into the dining room. 'I wasn't sure what to make, so I just made all of Olivia's favourites.' With a flourish, she revealed ten dishes with different meals arranged around the table. All of them vegetarian.

This could be a problem, Olivia thought.

She should have realised that there wouldn't be any meat on the menu at their house. 'There's plenty of iron in spinach,' Olivia whispered, knowing that wasn't going to help fill Ivy's stomach.

'Oh!' her mom exclaimed. 'I forgot the garlic bread!'

Oh no! Olivia thought. She remembered all too well what happened when Ivy ate even the tiniest amount of garlic – it was a full-scale vampire emergency.

Ivy sat down at her place with a forced smile on her face, but when Mrs Abbott went into the kitchen for the bread she leaned over the table and whispered, 'You're going to have to eat twice as much!'

'What?' Olivia asked.

'Your mom has gone to loads of effort. I can't leave tons of leftovers.'

Mrs Abbott came back and Ivy had to keep quiet. Mrs Abbott said brightly, 'Are you two girls going to spend all night talking about boys?'

'Mom,' Olivia complained.

'What's this about boys?' Mr Abbott said, walking into the room and sitting down.

'Nothing, Dad.' Olivia rolled her eyes.

'You know,' Mr Abbott said, stuffing his napkin into his shirt collar. 'I could help if you have boy troubles – I did use to be one, you know.'

Ivy chuckled. 'My boyfriend's trouble is that he's hungry all the time.'

'That's easy to fix!' Mr Abbott declared. 'Feed the boy!' And with that, he took a huge scoop of the mustard macaroni cheese in front of him.

Olivia watched as Ivy took a little bit of everything, a spoonful of the olive salad and the tiniest slice of the nut loaf. She could hear Ivy's stomach rumble and felt totally guilty.

Poor Ivy, Olivia thought.

'So what errand have you two sent Charles jetting off on?' Mr Abbott asked, taking three of the lotus-leaf parcels.

Mrs Abbott passed around the veggie dumplings. 'He said something about it being a trip for his daughters?'

The sisters exchanged a glance.

'We thought it was a business trip,' Olivia said.

'A piece of garlic bread, Ivy?' Mrs Abbott asked.

Olivia didn't have time to think about what her parents meant; she had to stop the garlic disaster! If any garlic so much as touched Ivy's plate, she wouldn't be able to eat a thing.

'Sure,' Ivy said brightly, trying to avoid touching any of the garlic butter. 'Thanks!'

Ivy was holding up the poisonous piece of bread, Mrs Abbott was waiting expectantly. Olivia had to do something.

'Um . . . can I smell something burning?' Olivia asked, sniffing the air.

'Oh no, did I leave the stove on?' Mrs Abbott rushed into the kitchen with Mr Abbott racing after her.

Ivy slipped her garlic bread on to Olivia's plate and carefully wiped her fingers on her napkin. 'Eat it quick!' Ivy said. 'They're coming back!'

Olivia shoved the whole slice of bread into her mouth as Mr and Mrs Abbott came back.

'Nothing burning,' Mrs Abbott confirmed.

Ivy made a big show of saying, 'Mmmm, garlic bread,' while Olivia tried to swallow the hunk of bread without choking. The edges of the crusts were scratching the inside of her cheeks and the salvia rushing into her mouth was making it hard not to dribble.

'Are you all right, Olivia?' Mrs Abbott asked.

Olivia could only nod emphatically and give the thumbs-up sign.

'Did you know there was a film crew in town?' Ivy put in while Olivia swallowed hard.

Olivia was on full alert for the rest of the meal and when her mom and dad disappeared into the kitchen to get dessert, Olivia clutched her tummy and groaned. 'I'm going to burst like a balloon.'

'I'm so sorry,' Ivy whispered back. 'But at

least you won't have to eat two desserts.'

'After all that garlic bread, I'm not going to be able to eat one dessert,' Olivia said.

Just then, there was a funny trumpeting noise from the kitchen and her mom and dad came back with party hats on and two candles in the middle of a pie.

They handed two matching party hats to the sisters that had 'Birthday' covered over with magazine letters cut out to read 'Happy Not Moving Day'.

'We know it should have been a couple of days ago,' Mrs Abbott said, 'but we wanted to recognise the wonderful news that you and your father aren't leaving.'

'Aw, thanks!' said Ivy, blowing out the candles.

'I'm full,' Olivia confessed when her mom offered her some delicious-looking lemon meringue pie.

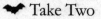

'But it's your favourite,' Mr Abbott said.

'I know, but –' Olivia began.

'Oh, sweetheart, it's a celebration!' said Mrs Abbott.

Olivia couldn't stand the upset look on her mother's face. She sighed. Her belly felt tight as a drum and a loud gurgle erupted. She hugged her stomach and tried to laugh.

'OK, maybe just a little,' she said, gazing at her plate as her mum slid a thick slice of trembling lemon meringue on to it.

'And as you girls have liked the garlic bread so much,' said Olivia's mom, picking up the empty plate, 'I'll make some more tomorrow!'

Ivy and Olivia looked at each other.

This might be a tricky few days! Olivia thought with dread.

Ivy was spread out like a bug splattered on a

windshield, trying to get comfortable on the air mattress that Olivia had blown up for her. But every movement felt squishy and wobbly – nothing at all like the cold, firm feel of a wooden coffin beneath her back, the pleasant feeling of being cosily encased.

'I can't get comfortable,' Ivy complained, pushing the fluffy pillow on to the shaggy white carpet and tugging at her flannel bat-covered pyjamas.

'At least you haven't been stuffed like a cabbage leaf,' Olivia groaned from her four-poster bed.

'Thanks for eating my share. I'll make it up to you, somehow.' Ivy wondered if she could block out the moonlight by taking the thick comforter and taping it up over the lace curtains on the window. *How do bunnies get* any *sleep?*

'It wasn't as bad as that time I had to face black pudding at your house – ugh!' Olivia said.

'You mean, yum,' Ivy said, her tummy grumbling. She wished she could sneak out of Olivia's bedroom window and go get a burger. 'Anyway, I've figured out the best way to show my appreciation for your deadly garlic breath: we go back to the movie set tomorrow and I get Jackson's autograph for you.'

Olivia sat up in her bed in her pink nightie and looked down at Ivy. 'He'd probably write: To Olivia, seek counselling, from Jackson. P.S. please keep at least 500 feet away from me.'

Ivy laughed. 'No, he wouldn't. I think he liked you. He went out of his way to ask your name. Besides, it would be totally killer for you to have a boyfriend, even if he wouldn't exactly be "perfectly normal" like you said you wanted.'

Olivia turned over on to her tummy, propping her chin on her hands. 'He asked Camilla her name, too. Besides, he's a movie star. Super-famous and super-talented and super-nice.'

'It was definitely love at first sight . . .' Ivy teased, 'of earmuffs.'

'I just wish I hadn't been such a dork when he came over,' Olivia said, flopping down dramatically.

Ivy realised her mission shouldn't be to get Olivia an autograph but to find her a second chance to make a first impression. 'Let's just see what happens tomorrow,' she said, lying back down on the mattress. But with every shift, the mattress squeaked and Ivy knew it would take eternity to fall asleep like this. Maybe she could sleep on the floor?

'You are squeaking like a bat on that thing.' Olivia climbed out of her bed. 'I think I know what might work.'

Olivia cleared off the hair brushes, perfumes and accessories from her extra-long white wooden dressing table. 'If you used this as a

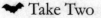

mattress, it might feel like a coffin.'

'Genius!' Ivy declared. 'You are the best sister.'

As quietly as they could, they shifted the mirror safely off and carefully flipped the dressing table over so its legs were up in the air. Ivy lay on the upside down table and folded her arms. 'Aaah.' The moon was still shining in through the window, but with the hard wood against her shoulder blades, the faint smell of the forest, and coldness under her head, it was almost like being at home.

Olivia dragged over the air mattress and propped it up against the wall at an angle over Ivy's head. 'My own makeshift bat cave,' Ivy said appreciatively. It wasn't her coffin, but it would definitely work. 'Good night, Olivia.'

'Good night, my unusual roommate.'

Ivy could hear her climbing back into bed.

As Ivy drifted off, she ran through scenarios

of how she could get Olivia and Jackson to talk to each other again. Maybe she and Olivia could sneak on to the set disguised as bushes? Or pretend to be singing telegrams? Maybe she could put her sister in a suitcase marked for special delivery to Jackson? On second thoughts, that really might land them with a restraining order.

Ivy was determined it was her turn to play matchmaker. *I'll make this happen*, she swore. *One way or another . . .*

🦇   🦇   🦇

Olivia was woken by Ivy bouncing on her bed. 'What bunny magic has made you so chirpy?' she groaned as she peered through her half-awake eyes.

'Tai chi with your dad,' said Ivy, who had developed a refreshing glow. 'I feel amazing! Energised and enlightened!'

'Can you be enlightened somewhere else

please? I'm trying to sleep.' Olivia pulled the duvet over her head, but she was only teasing; she loved seeing her twin getting on with her family.

'Hey, I thought I was supposed to be the grumpy one, remember?'

Olivia pushed back the covers and sat up straight. With a huge grin she said, 'That's right! Let's call Sophia and we'll have a full-on girlie morning!'

'Awesome!' said Ivy, jumping up in an uncharacteristic cheerleading pose.

Sophia was over within half an hour. Sophia and Ivy, declaring themselves Olivia's stylist team, debated over what Olivia should wear for her second meeting with Jackson, and settled on a light blue sweater with denim shorts and lacy leggings.

Then they had a quick hair and make-up session. Olivia did Ivy's nails with Diva at Dusk blue-black and Sophia chose Vampy Violet. Olivia covered her own in Just Peachy. It meant they had to eat their scrambled eggs carefully, holding their forks so that they wouldn't smear the varnish.

As they left Olivia put on her glittery earmuffs.

'Jackson's favourite accessory!' Ivy teased.

But Olivia ignored her. 'Bright red, frozen ears only look good on elves,' she announced.

They headed out of the door for the Meat & Greet.

Ivy continued to talk about Jackson. 'What if we rented a helicopter and dropped you inside? Jackson would be impressed by that.'

Or I would break my neck and be rushed to hospital, Olivia thought.

'As long as I don't have to chip in to pay for it,' Sophia said.

'That won't be necessary,' Olivia replied.

'Besides, I'm going back to the set to learn about movies, not stalk the male lead.'

'Is that . . . is your nose . . .' Ivy was peering at Olivia's face. 'Is your nose growing, Pinocchio?'

Olivia poked her tongue out and gently pushed her sister away.

Jackson coming to Franklin Grove was the most exciting thing that had ever happened to Olivia, but making a fool of herself in front of him was one of the worst. She just wanted to put the whole thing behind her.

The three girls turned the corner to the Meat & Greet and staggered to a halt. In front of them was a crowd bigger than the biggest pep rally Olivia had ever seen. And the noise! It looked like every girl within twenty miles had gathered around the barriers. Some were even holding signs. One had the very unoriginal, 'Marry me, Jackson,' but another had an illustration of a jack from a deck of cards, then a picture of the sun, then an equals sign and a big red heart after that. Cute. *Jackson equals love*. The girl with the pink and blue polka-dot jacket from yesterday was still right at the front. Her hair was a lot messier and Olivia wondered if she'd even been home.

'So, it looks like the word's out,' Sophia said drily.

'Hmm,' Ivy said, surveying the huge crowd. 'How are we going to get in now?'

'Got to be the helicopter or nothing,' Sophia replied.

'Have you heard about the side entrance?' a familiar voice said behind them.

Olivia and Ivy whipped around to see Brendan wearing his black trench coat and a sneaky grin.

'No,' Ivy said, giving him a quick hug hello. 'Tell us!'

'What's in it for me?' he said.

'How about a rare burger on me when the Meat & Greet opens again?' Ivy offered.

'Sold!' Brendan said, shaking Ivy's hand in an official way. 'Come on. Follow me.' He led them around the crowd to the side of the parking lot. There were only a handful of spectators gathered by these barriers: an older lady in a scruffy coat, two men with big Jackson posters, and a mom with two excited little girls. Three security guards stood with their arms crossed, keeping an eye out for anyone trying to sneak in.

'Since it doesn't look like much is happening,' Brendan said, 'I'm going to head to the Juice Bar. Anybody want anything?'

'I'm starving.' Ivy clung to Brendan's arm. 'Food at the Abbott's is . . . um . . . a little light for me.'

Olivia and Ivy had already planned to sneak a roast-beef sandwich for Ivy to eat after dinner tonight, and to say Ivy had a tummy ache so that Olivia wouldn't have to eat twice as much.

'How about a Breakfast Bun with Bite?' Brendan asked.

'Ooh, with extra red sauce.' The excitement on Ivy's face made Olivia smile. *They are so cute together*, Olivia thought.

'And a blood orange juice?' Brendan offered.

'My hero!' Ivy said, batting her lashes like a damsel in distress.

As Brendan left, Olivia realised that one of the security guards was Jerome, their friend from yesterday. She waved until she caught his attention and he came a little closer to the barrier. 'Thanks so much for the heads up yesterday.'

'No problem,' he said, tipping his Harker Films baseball hat.

'Any chance of some insider info today?' Ivy asked.

'Sorry, ladies.' He lowered his glasses and shrugged. 'I've got nothing for you. Being on barrier duty means I don't know what's happening on the inside.'

'Thanks anyway.' Olivia shrugged in an effort not to look stalker-ish.

'Now can we try the helicopter?' Ivy whispered.

Olivia held a finger to her lips. She jerked her head in the direction of the other two security guards. 'Listen,' she hissed. 'I think that guy is talking about Jackson.'

'What is the big deal with this Caulfield kid?' the shorter guard was saying. 'He's probably just some pretty boy with fewer brain cells than a jellyfish.'

His taller companion in a hat and sunglasses replied with a strong English accent, 'I hear he works pretty hard at what he does.'

His friend continued, 'Bah! He doesn't know

the meaning of hard work. We're the ones standing out here in the freezing cold! These boys are a dime a dozen; he'll fade away into obscurity.'

Olivia could feel her toes curling up with anger – how dare the man say these things? 'Excuse me,' she called over. The two security guards turned in her direction while Jerome leaned on the barrier near the girls. 'It's really not fair to judge someone you don't know.'

The short man took off his sunglasses. 'I was just saying –'

Ivy put a hand on her arm, but Olivia wasn't going to be dissuaded. 'You were just being pretty mean about a guy you don't even know.'

The guards all stared at her.

'Are you going to make the effort to actually get to know Jackson,' Olivia went on, 'or will you just end up spreading around ideas that he's not a good person, simply because of what he does?'

'Listen, kid,' the short man said. 'I don't know who you are, but I don't give two hoots what you think about Jackson. Now, get out of here!'

'Come on!' Ivy pulled her sister away before things could get any worse.

'Wh-what?' Olivia said, almost tripping over her faux-fur boots.

Even when they were a safe distance away opposite one of the big trucks, Ivy and Sophia had to stand between Olivia and the guards, she was so ready to go back and keep talking.

'You're going to start a lynch mob,' Ivy said.

'Did you see that lady behind us?' Sophia pointed to the large lady in the coat. 'She was about to jump in and give that guard a piece of her mind, too.'

'We're trying to get you a second chance to see Jackson, not get thrown off the set,' Ivy scolded.

This matchmaking thing was turning out to be more difficult than she'd expected.

'Pardon me,' said the voice with the English accent. Spinning round, Ivy saw the taller security guard. His hat, sunglasses and turned-up collar covered most of his face.

Uh oh, Ivy thought. I bet he's going to make us leave the premises.

'Yes?' she asked, shoving Olivia behind her to prevent her saying anything else. *Maybe I can talk our way out of this*, Ivy thought.

'I just wanted to say: don't worry about Harry,' the man said. 'He was born grumpy.'

Olivia stepped out from behind Ivy. 'I didn't mean to be rude; I just wanted him to know how wrong he was.'

'Those earmuffs look smashing, by the way.' The security guard smiled.

'Uh, thanks,' Olivia said, her hand moving to

touch one of the muffs.

'Sorry,' Ivy said. 'We didn't mean any harm.'

But the security guard wasn't listening to Ivy; he stepped closer to Olivia and said, 'I should be thanking you.'

'What for?' Olivia asked.

He slid his glasses down his nose and Ivy could see a light of recognition in Olivia's eyes.

'Olivia, do you know him?' Ivy asked, staring. Then she caught sight of the guard's sparkling blue eyes.

Ivy pointed and said, 'You're, you're . . .'

Sophia slapped her hand away and said, 'Don't blow it!'

The security man was Jackson.

Chapter Four

'Hi there,' Jackson said, dropping the English accent. 'Nice to see you again, Olivia.'

He remembers my name! Olivia thought.

'Um, nice to see you, too.'

Jackson's disguise was so complete, with the heavy boots and walkie-talkie; he even had the muscled arms to fill out the uniform. 'I never would have guessed it was you,' she said, wondering why he would want to be mistaken for a security guard.

'How about I take you and your two friends

on a quick tour of the set?' he offered, pushing his sunglasses up his nose. 'To say thank you for standing up to Harry for me.'

'That would be killer!' Sophia said.

'Quick, through here!' Jackson pulled away one of the plastic barriers just enough for them to slip through. He looked over his shoulder to make sure no one was watching. 'Get behind that truck!'

As Olivia ducked through first, Jackson whispered. 'Don't draw any attention to us or we'll get swamped.'

'What about Brendan?' Ivy said as they stepped past the barriers.

'We'll meet up with him later,' Sophia said, pushing her own way through. 'Come on!'

Ivy and Sophia scurried behind the back of the truck, but as Olivia followed them she stumbled over the base of the hollow plastic barrier, making a loud thump. She fell against Jackson with a muffled squeak. In an instant, his strong arms wrapped around her waist and pulled her behind the truck. So much for not drawing any attention. *Why am I such a goof ball in front of Jackson?* Olivia thought.

'I think we got away with it,' Jackson said, risking a glance around the truck. He was still gently holding her arm. He noticed her looking down at his hand and pulled away. Olivia found herself loosening her knitted rainbow scarf.

'Warm?' Ivy asked.

Sophia grinned. 'Despite the frost?'

Olivia shook her head, yanking at the scarf. 'It's all the excitement.'

'The excitement?' Ivy said, raising her eyebrows and directing a pointed look at Jackson.

'I mean of sneaking in!' Olivia hissed, digging an elbow into her sister's ribs.

'OK, ladies,' Jackson said. 'If you follow me, I will start your personal tour. There are a few safety procedures I must run through,' he said, taking on an official tone. 'In the unlikely event of a fire just leap over the barriers and run for it . . . and please don't leave me behind.'

Olivia giggled.

He strode confidently out into the buzzing parking lot and the girls hurried to keep up.

'This is so awesome!' Sophia said.

Olivia was still wondering what made him get all dressed up. 'Why the disguise?' she asked.

Jackson steered them between two trailers, going deeper into the maze of trucks. 'It gets really boring on set when you're not filming.'

'I can't imagine getting bored on a movie set,' Sophia replied.

Me neither, Olivia thought as a young man carried a stack of big cardboard posters with little squares laid out like a comic book.

Jackson noticed what she was looking at and explained. 'Those are the storyboards. It's the scene by scene plan of how the director wants the movie to look.'

'So that blue blob sitting in the booth is you?' Ivy asked.

Jackson chuckled. 'Yes, this is a romantic comedy between two sketchy blobs.'

'Love truly is universal,' Ivy said, pretending to be philosophical and looking at Olivia and winking.

'Ha ha,' Olivia said, doing her best to give her sister a death stare.

I wish Ivy would stop teasing, Olivia thought. *It's hard enough not to do anything else stupid, without being constantly reminded how much I like him.*

'To answer your question,' Jackson continued, 'after my third movie, I had gotten used to all the movie madness. Plus a disguise lets me meet people without all the entourage and shrieking.' He looked at Olivia and smiled.

Her heart fluttered.

'It's nice to be normal again, every once in a while,' he finished.

Jackson pointed to a tent on their left. 'There's the props tent and down there is one of the costume trailers on the right.'

Olivia heard Ivy and Sophia whispering behind her, but she was determined to ignore them. Jackson wanted to be normal, so she was just going to pretend she was with a normal – but really nice – security guard.

'This is so much fun,' Olivia said. Walking around a movie set with Jackson Caulfield was even better than cheering at nationals.

'That guy in the black is the boom operator. And she's the continuity editor.' Jackson leaned in close as he pointed to show her who he meant. 'And that guy, right there? In the white shirt and jeans?' Near the props tent, a guy was slouched on a crate. 'That's my twin.'

Olivia gasped. 'Really? You're a twin?'

'Not really. He's my stand-in,' Jackson explained. 'When they're setting up camera angles and lighting, he takes my place so they can see how it will look when they film me. Basically, it gives me free time to snoop around the set in disguise.'

Olivia was about to point out her and Ivy's twin-ness but then Jackson's red-headed manager stormed up to them. Her high heels clipped sharply on the concrete. Her tailored grey skirt suit had tiny pink pinstripes running down it and her spiky high heels were patent grey leather with a pink bow. Olivia could read 'Amy Teller' on her all-access badge.

'You there!' Amy barked at Jackson.

'Caught red-handed,' Olivia muttered.

'Sshh,' Jackson said, pulling his hat down.

'You! Security! Have you seen Jackson?' Amy demanded, looking him right in the eyes. Well, right in the sunglasses.

Jackson cleared his throat. 'Who's Jackson?' he replied in his English accent.

Amy stamped her foot and sighed. 'The star of the film you are working on!'

Olivia tried hard not to laugh.

'No, madam,' he said.

Amy blinked, not recognising Jackson at all. 'This boy is going to turn my hair grey,' she muttered as she strode off.

'Her hair is already grey,' Jackson said, as he watched her leave. 'She gets it touched up every six weeks.'

Olivia was finally able to laugh. 'That was

close.' She was surprised that Ivy hadn't already made some killer comment about the woman's thunderous expression. 'Hey, Ivy – did you see the look on that woman's face?' She turned to her sister, but ended up turning in a full circle. 'Ivy?' There was nothing in a two-foot radius other than thin air. Her sister was gone!

Olivia met Jackson's eye.

'Looks like it's just you and me,' Jackson said, smiling.

Olivia's heart did a triple handspring.

🦇   🦇   🦇

'Mission accomplished,' Ivy declared. She had pulled Sophia behind the props tent when Olivia wasn't looking.

This will work, Ivy thought. *A little time alone should get those sparks flying.*

Now she and Sophia were walking towards the Meat & Greet to get a closer look at the set.

81

'Do you think Olivia will be OK?' Sophia wondered.

'As long as she doesn't go blurting out phrases from the Wild West,' Ivy replied. She adjusted her black, coffin-shaped messenger bag. 'Honestly, Olivia and Jackson are like Romeo and Juliet – meant to be together!' Ivy remembered how Jackson only had eyes for Olivia when they'd first met, and again at the barrier. They did seem to be a great fit, except for Olivia wanting a 'perfectly normal' boyfriend. 'Anyway, now that we're on a movie set, shouldn't we do some skulking around?'

Sophia's eyes lit up. 'Ooh, could we actually get into the diner?'

'Whoa, Miss Eager Reaper! Let's not push our luck,' Ivy replied. 'Rather than sneaking to where they're filming, how about checking out the equipment area over there?' There were cameras and complicated-looking electrical boards under a shade, gathered at the side entrance to the diner. *Maybe after that*, Ivy thought, *we could try and scrounge some food from somewhere*. She was still craving something meaty for breakfast.

The vampire girls strolled over, trying to pretend they were exactly where they were supposed to be.

A woman with a tight bun and a clipboard walked by. She peered at everything and made notes to herself. Ivy held her breath, but the woman just glanced at them and kept walking.

We're in, Ivy thought.

'Oh my darkness,' Sophia said.

'What?' Ivy said, looking around.

'That is an Xtra Vision LT-2K high definition digital camera with interchangeable optical assembly, a touch screen interface and four hours of continuous shooting.' Sophia sighed and practically floated towards the very-expensive-looking piece of equipment.

'Um, Sophia?' But her friend was already reaching out a hand to the camera, stroking its digital screen.

The neon danger sign in the back of Ivy's mind had started flashing and she stepped forward to stop her. 'Sophia –'

'Hey, you girls!'

Ivy froze at the sound of a stern voice and Sophia whipped around, almost knocking the camera over.

'Maybe we should have stayed with Jackson,' Ivy whispered and turned slowly to face the music.

'Where are your set passes?' said a pale, thin woman with frizzy black hair poking out from underneath a pair of over-sized headphones.

Ivy and Sophia stood guilty and silent. *It was*

fun while it lasted, Ivy thought.

'You aren't supposed to be here, are you?' the woman asked in a thick New York accent.

Ivy shook her head.

'I don't know why we don't make maps for reception to give out. Honestly!'

'Huh?' said Sophia.

But Ivy nodded cautiously. *Maybe we aren't going to get completely staked*, she thought.

The woman looked them both over. 'Hmmm. Yes, I can see why they picked you two – the alternative style, the nice faces. Good.'

Ivy looked at Sophia, who seemed just as confused.

'I'm Lillian, the second assistant director.' She checked her watch. 'Come with me and I'll get you to the extras trailer.'

The extras trailer? Ivy thought.

Lillian started to walk away.

'Does this mean we're going to be *in* the movie?' Ivy asked Sophia.

'I think so!' Sophia almost skipped after the woman and Ivy hurried to keep up.

Ivy normally hated the spotlight, but this wasn't centre stage. She was only going to be in the background. Killer!

'Get your rears in gear, ladies,' Lillian said. 'We've got to get you ready for blocking the first set-up.'

Ivy had no idea what she was talking about, but Sophia whispered, 'That means planning out how the actors will move in a scene.'

'Thank darkness you're here to translate,' Ivy said.

They marched up to a big trailer labelled 'Background Artists' and Lillian handed over two location passes, then thumped on the door.

'Two more for ya, Spencer!'

A man with closely shaved dark hair and stubble opened the door. His blue silk shirt was unbuttoned half way down his chest and he was wearing heeled leather shoes. He put one hand on his hip and looked the girls up and down. He gasped and put the other hand to his forehead. 'Oh my goodness. What am I going to do with you two?' He had a slight lisp and spoke really quickly. 'You simply must get in here right away.'

He turned on his heel and disappeared inside. Lillian hurried off before Ivy could thank her.

They stepped tentatively into the trailer to see about a dozen people their age getting their hair and make-up done.

'Wait there,' Spencer commanded, pointing to two black leather chairs in front of brightly lit mirrors. He flitted away to the other side of the trailer to rummage through a tall organiser, muttering to himself.

'This utterly sucks!' Ivy declared, leaning back in the comfy chair. Today could not be going any better.

I hope Olivia's having as much fun as me, Ivy thought.

'Is this your first time?' asked a boy in layered T-shirts next to her.

Ivy nodded.

Spencer came back with a tray of tubes, jars and brushes. He put a finger to his lips and cocked his head on one side, considering. Ivy felt her cheeks start to blush under the scrutiny. Then he clapped his hands together, as though he'd come to a decision.

'Now, we're not going to do much to your hair – long and luxurious, well done, sweetie.' Ivy smiled. 'But we are going to have to brighten the skin tone for both of you. And I was thinking a teased up-do for you,' he said to Sophia. She gave him a shaky smile.

He snapped his fingers and a hairdresser stepped forward and started to work on Sophia. Then Spencer whipped out a cleanser. Ivy couldn't believe she was getting pampered by a professional movie-set make-up artist.

Spencer grabbed for a Mister Smoothie pink and yellow cup from the ledge in front of the mirror and took a big slurp.

'What flavour did you get?' Ivy asked as he worked.

'Ooh,' Spencer said. 'I heard the Twist and Shout was a sight to see, so I just had to go for that one!'

Ivy cracked up. 'My dad ordered that yesterday.'

Spencer's eyes widened. 'Your *dad*? Ha!' Spencer started doing a fabulous hip twist. 'Us older men love to dance! Once the rest of the crew heard about the little show, they've been ordering them all day. LOVE it!' Spencer did a triple-zigzag finger snap.

Ivy felt a twinge of pity for the Mister Smoothie staff.

'You are truly beautiful,' he said to Ivy, gently wiping a cleansing pad across her brow. 'Your friend, too. But you are both so *pale*. This foundation isn't going to be enough. Lucky for us, we have enough fake tan on set for the star of the show to last through the sequel!'

Something niggled at the back of Ivy's mind. *Lots of fake tan?*

'Georgie!' Spencer called and a young girl with teased up-hair in a flowing crushed velvet dress came over. 'Can you go get me a couple cans of the Santa Monica, please?'

As Georgie scurried off, Ivy felt a sense of

dread rising. Santa Monica was *the* fake tan of choice for the vampire community.

'For the star?' Ivy squeaked out.

Spencer nodded. 'The contract rider demanded at least three cases of the top range of Santa Monica spray tan.'

Ivy felt her stomach churn. She thought of Jackson's peachy complexion – if he was human and put on that spray tan, he'd look like an orange. But he didn't; he looked completely normal. Completely human. Which meant that without fake tan his skin must be really, really pale. Could Jackson be . . .

'A vampire,' Ivy whispered.

'Pardon?' Spencer asked, his pad of cleanser freezing in mid-air.

'Oh, nothing,' Ivy said, lowering her eyes.

'Are you OK?' Sophia asked.

'I – I've got to go find Olivia,' Ivy blurted,

trying to get up from the chair. She couldn't let her sister fall for a vampire. Olivia wouldn't want that at all; she'd said so herself. Ivy had to tell her before it was too late.

But Spencer put a hand on her shoulder. 'Slow down, honey. You're not going anywhere until you're camera-ready.'

'But I –'

'Ah, ah, ah!' Spencer wagged his finger right in her face and wouldn't let her go.

Ivy sighed and sank back into the chair.

'What's wrong?' Sophia hissed, leaning over the side of her chair.

Ivy swallowed hard and tried to give her friend a smile. 'Nothing!' she said brightly. She wouldn't be able to share her fears until they were alone again. 'Everything is just peachy!'

Chapter Five

I hope Ivy's having as much fun as me, Olivia thought. At first she'd been really freaked out that Ivy had left her alone with Jackson, but he was making her feel so at ease.

'And this is Craft Service,' Jackson said, standing at the opening of a huge eighteen-wheeler which was well lit with flood lamps and smelled delicious. 'Translation: the cafeteria.'

It was much warmer in the truck than outside. Long tables were set out with enough food to feed four hungry high schools. There was a line of people carrying steaming plates and cooks tending to various portable stoves. It looked like a mobile gourmet restaurant.

'I thought we'd stop for a snack,' Jackson said. 'It's almost my call time, and it might kill the mood if my stomach growls during filming.'

'You're the tour guide,' Olivia said, 'where you lead, I'll follow.' Then she blushed as she realised that she sounded stalker-y again. But Jackson didn't seem to notice and he directed her to a line behind some crew members.

The chefs were serving out everything from duck salad to pasta with truffles to fancy-looking mini-pizzas, and even rows of sushi on ice.

'You can have whatever you like,' Jackson offered, but Olivia still felt full from last night.

'Maybe I'll just have a fruit cup,' she said to the grey-haired cook with a wrinkly but friendly face, whose name badge said 'Curtis'. 'I had a big breakfast.'

'As you wish.' Curtis shrugged and handed over a small plastic bowl filled with fresh, colourful fruit pieces.

When it was his turn, Jackson pulled down his shades so Curtis could see who he was. Curtis laughed. 'Right on time, as usual.'

Curtis turned the dial on a small microwave nearby. 'You know,' he said in his gravelly voice, 'people will catch on to your disappearing act eventually. Your manager has stormed through here twice looking for you.'

'You wouldn't give away my secret, would you?' Jackson replied.

'Course not,' Curtis said. 'How else would I supply my daughter with Jackson Caulfield memorabilia?'

The microwave dinged and Curtis pulled out a burger in a little paper tray. He leaned over and mock-whispered, 'One hunk of cow smothered in cheese waiting just for you.'

Olivia crinkled her nose. It was the only thing about Jackson this whole morning that surprised her; it looked like Jackson's taste buds were more in line with Ivy's than her own. She couldn't help feeling it made him a little less . . . perfect.

They sat down at a table between some crew members and a group of younger girls and Jackson tucked into his burger. Olivia didn't want to watch him eating, so she looked around at all the people munching away in the back of this gigantic truck: people in all black, people in full make-up and tired-looking people poring over stacks of papers.

'Tell me about you,' Jackson said, between mouthfuls.

'What do you want to know?' Olivia asked. She plucked a juicy piece of orange from her fruit cup.

'What's your favourite movie?'

Olivia looked back down at her bowl to hide her face. She didn't want to confess that it was one of his. 'I, um, love so many. I couldn't pick just one.'

'What about books, then?' he asked, wiping the back of his hand across his mouth.

That one was easy. 'I'm a huge Count Vira fan,' she replied.

'I love those, too!' He put on a thick Transylvanian accent. 'Come to me, my darling, and I will take your breath away.'

Olivia recognised that line from *Thrice Bitten*. She knew the next line, too. 'But what about my employers?' she said breathlessly.

Jackson smiled as he played along. 'They will not miss you, my love. I am your destiny!'

Olivia giggled. 'I love that story.'

'Me, too,' Jackson said.

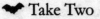

Olivia bit her lip. *We like the same books!* she thought.

The girls next to them burst into squeals.

'I can't believe we're extras on the same movie set as Jackson Caulfield,' the one with brown pigtails said. 'He is sooo gorgeous!'

'What if we get to be in a scene with him?' replied the girl with a blue streak in her hair.

'I know how we can definitely meet him,' said the third girl wearing a cute bucket hat. 'We should wait around outside his trailer and pretend to be lost when he shows up.'

Olivia had to shove a piece of watermelon in her mouth to stop from laughing. The girls had no idea they were sitting right next to Jackson. He looked at her over his sunglasses and winked.

She was having such a good time with him. If it weren't for the fan girls, it would almost be like Jackson was just a normal guy – not a famous movie star. Olivia wondered for a moment what would happen if he were just a regular person. Would they have a chance together?

'But we'll have to make sure we don't run into *her*,' said Brown Pigtails.

'Ugh, no,' said Bucket Hat. 'She's *such* a diva!'

'I heard she's already fired three hairdressers and two caterers and insisted on bringing in her own,' said Blue Streak.

'Who are they talking about?' Olivia whispered to Jackson, who had thankfully moved on to eating his fries.

'That would be my co-star.' Jackson shrugged. 'Jessica Phelps. But I bet if you ask her, she doesn't have a co-star.'

Jessica Phelps had shot to fame being cast as the lead girl in a New York fashion movie. She was on the cover of every magazine, including this issue of *Celeb Weekly*. Olivia realised what a big deal this production must be, with two such huge stars in it. 'What's the movie about, anyway?'

Jackson's face lit up. 'It's such a great concept! As soon as I heard the pitch I wanted to sign up. It's called *The Groves* and it opens with a guy named Chase on vacation, falling in love with another tourist named Mia. After a wonderful date on the beach, her parents whisk her away before he can get her phone number. He can't stop thinking about her, and all he knows is that she lives in Franklin Grove. Trouble is: there are five Franklin Groves all over America. He sets out with three friends on a road trip to visit every one until he finds her. In each Franklin Grove, he imagines what it will be like when he finally finds her. We're filming the first imaginary meeting today.'

Olivia found herself swept up in the story. 'That sounds so romantic.' His enthusiasm about it made him even more charming. 'I can't wait to see it.'

'You won't have to,' he replied. 'It's being rushed out before the end of the school year. There's even talk of filming a sequel in the fall.'

Olivia frowned. 'Does that mean Chase and Mia don't end up together?'

'Now that would be telling . . .'

Jackson's walkie talkie crackled and Amy's exasperated voice came over the speaker: 'J. C. starts shooting in half an hour. If *any*one sees him, they are to escort him to his trailer immediately!'

'Whoops, that's my cue.' Jackson shoved the last two fries into his mouth. 'I better go let someone turn me in.' Olivia felt her heart drop. Her personal tour was over. 'I always have to have extra time in make-up to touch up my tan.'

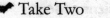

'Don't you Hollywood types spend all day in the sun?' Olivia teased.

'I'm not really a big fan of the beach or the sun,' Jackson confessed. 'I've even been thinking of buying a house away from the baking heat of Beverly Hills.'

Olivia had had one of the best mornings of her life, and she didn't want it to end. Just as she was taking a breath to say goodbye, Jackson reached into a jacket pocket and handed her a plastic laminated pass that read, 'VIP Guest'.

He took off his sunglasses and pulled down his hat, turning away from everybody as much as he could. His blue eyes were mesmerising. 'Please don't go just yet. This pass will get you in anywhere. Stay and watch the filming.'

An all-access pass! 'Of course,' she said, trying hard not to hug herself with delight.

Then he put his sunglasses back on and strode

away, giving her a little wave as he hopped down from the truck. No one gave him a second glance. Olivia sat for a moment, staring at her shiny pass. She had basically just had a private lunch with one of the biggest stars in Hollywood, but there had been times when things felt completely normal. Could he possibly be the guy she'd been waiting for?

Don't be ridiculous, she told herself. Jackson was super-famous and he would never really be interested in her. He was just being nice.

Time to find Ivy, Olivia thought. Olivia hurried out into the cold air and tried to call her twin, but Ivy's phone was off. She'd just have to look for her. Clutching her new pass, she set off, hoping that Ivy hadn't already been discovered and chucked off set.

As she passed a row of trailers, a bald man grabbed her hands and twirled her around. 'Oh, yes, sweetie!' he exclaimed. 'I am good. Your skin tone looks flawless in this light. Gorgeous!' He did a triple-zigzag finger snap and then he sashayed away.

Olivia had no idea who he was or what he was talking about. But being called gorgeous by a perfect stranger was enough to make her extra-special day . . . well . . . perfect.

'Background artists, please,' called a man wearing headphones with earpieces that were bigger than a Meat & Greet burger. He darted back into the diner and Lillian shooed the group of fashionably dressed teens up the steps and inside. One girl was wearing a white wool wrap-around with rainbow-coloured buttons and another had on a deep purple slash-neck sweater. They looked like they'd just stepped out of a jeans commercial.

'It's not like they're going to get married before lunch,' Sophia was saying. 'You can tell her your theory when we see her later – and it's only a *theory*.'

'But if Olivia really falls for him –' Ivy began.

'Come on, Ivy, you don't have any proof.' Sophia nudged her along with the crowd. She was looking killer with her messy up-do and long-sleeved, black tube dress. It was the first time Ivy had seen her oldest friend with a necklace rather than a camera around her neck.

Ivy had loved every second of sifting through the extras rack in the costume trailer. For herself, she had chosen a triple-layered loose knit sweater with grey, mauve and black on top of each other over a pair of black jeans. She'd made friends with the jewellery assistant who'd lent her a set of heavy silver bracelets that clunked as she moved. Awesome.

But something was threatening to spoil the fun, like a cloud of darkness hovering. Olivia had said straight as a stake that she didn't want to date a vampire.

If I have just set Olivia up with a vampire, she could end up broken-hearted, Ivy thought. *And it would be all my fault.*

Ivy was following the group across the diner, mulling it over in her head.

'Hey, watch it!' Sophia grabbed Ivy, startling her. 'Look!' Sophia pointed at the ground.

Ivy was just about to step into a tangle of wires on the floor.

Lillian hurried over. 'Disaster averted. Thank you,' she said to Sophia. 'If you'd pulled on those wires –' Lillian indicated the lights above – 'all of those would have come crashing down.'

'Ohmygosh,' Ivy replied. 'I'm so sorry!' Ivy wouldn't want to do anything to get in trouble on set. Or ruin the set.

Sophia tugged Ivy around the equipment safely.

The production team had moved away all the normal diner booths except for the back row and one in front, obviously where the stars were going to sit.

'You, purple sweater, sit there,' Lillian said as she arranged the twenty or so extras in groups around the tables. 'And you, T-shirt boy, you're there.'

Ivy and Sophia got to sit together at a booth all the way on the right. When Lillian plunked some fake food in front of them, Ivy's stomach churned – she still hadn't had anything decent to eat. The plastic burger was starting to look tempting.

'Now, remember,' Lillian instructed. 'You pretend to be talking whenever the cameras roll.'

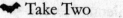

She opened and closed her mouth soundlessly. '*Pretend*, got it?'

Lillian stood back and then frowned. 'Hold up! We're missing one. Where did that blonde go?'

The door to the Meat & Greet flew open and everyone turned to look. Ivy and Sophia gasped but no one else paid any attention. Charlotte Brown, wearing an outrageous blue feathered dress, clicked her way over to Lillian in super-high heels. She looked like she was going to prom.

'She must be freezing,' Sophia commented.

'Sorry I'm late. The costume department couldn't find anything that was right, so I had to do some emergency shopping.' She did a twirl, not noticing the disdain on Lillian's face.

Lillian crossed her arms. 'Don't you think that's a bit over the top for a diner, missy?'

'Oh, I wear this sort of thing all the time.' Charlotte waved her hand, but almost slipped out of her strappy heel.

Ivy sensed trouble brewing. Charlotte had obviously figured out that the Meat and Greet was not closed down because of a sewer problem and, once she spotted Ivy, there would be retaliation. *How did she manage to get on set so quickly?* Ivy wondered as she slunk down in her seat and let her hair fall over her face.

Lillian stuck Charlotte next to a guy wearing a beanie and cargo pants, almost as far from the camera as she could. Ivy sat up a little; Charlotte couldn't see her from where she was sitting.

'*Non, non, non!*' shouted a small man with a goatee and a heavy French accent. 'The colours, the colours!'

'Sorry, Philippe,' Lillian said. 'I could –'

But he waved his hand in her face. He strode

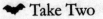

over and started yanking people up from their tables and rearranging them. Ivy realised he was the director and perhaps needed a good six months at a yoga retreat to find some inner peace. Philippe was like a grumpy fly, buzzing at everyone.

He marched over to Charlotte's table. 'You, in that blue!'

'*Moi?*' Charlotte sounded like she thought he was going to give her the starring role.

'Take it off!'

'Wh-what?' Charlotte spluttered.

Ivy and Sophia – along with several other extras – leaned over to see what was happening.

'*Non, non.* You will distract the eye.' He snapped his fingers and pointed at a grey jacket on the back of his director's chair. The man with the headphones scurried over with it and

Philippe tossed the jacket at Charlotte. 'Put this on and come with me.'

A miserable Charlotte did as she was told and scooted out of the booth. He grabbed her hand and dragged her to a different table, as she stumbled and tried to keep up.

Ivy looked away but not in time. Charlotte caught sight of her and shot a death stare that Ivy would have been proud of . . . if she hadn't been on the receiving end of it.

'Uh oh,' Sophia said. 'Busted.'

'She can't do anything now,' Ivy whispered back. 'She wouldn't risk it.'

Once Charlotte was installed at the next table over, grey and drab, the director clapped his hands. 'Where are my actors? Where? *Where?*' He threw himself into his chair and covered his eyes with his hands.

The diner door opened again and Jackson

strolled in right on cue, script in hand. There was no sign of Olivia; Ivy wondered what that meant. Maybe their private tour had been awful and Olivia decided she wasn't interested after all. That would bring a swift end to Ivy's matchmaking disaster. *I hope she's OK*, Ivy thought.

Philippe leapt from his chair, gesticulating at Jackson. 'This! I do not believe this. Don't you know your lines?'

Jackson slapped the papers into Philippe's flailing hand. 'Like a warlock knows his spells. I'm completely off-script.'

'That's vamp slang,' Ivy hissed.

'I'd call that wizard slang, really,' Sophia whispered back.

'But he was so calm,' Ivy argued. He was keeping his cool, just like a vampire.

'He must be used to all kinds of crazy directors,' Sophie countered.

Jackson noticed them staring and gave a little wave to her and Sophia. *What if he heard us talking about him with his super vamp hearing?* Ivy thought. *Hmm. I could test him.*

'Sophia,' Ivy whispered as quietly as she could, keeping a close eye on Jackson. 'I heard Jackson gets manicures.' She was making it up, but she thought it might get a reaction if he overheard.

'What are you talking about?' Sophia asked, but Ivy was watching Jackson.

Did he flinch? Ivy couldn't be sure. But he kept his cool with the director, maybe he was using his acting skills to remain straight-faced?

He continued to run through some lines with a stand-in. Ivy cursed the fact that vampires could blend in so easily – she couldn't tell if he was or wasn't just by looking at him. And she could hardly trail him until he went to the BloodMart –

with his legions of fans, he would have iron-clad avoidance tactics.

Sophia pushed a napkin over, with a little cartoon scribbled on it. There was an angry-looking man with a goatee shouting at a group of frightened stick figures. Ivy snorted when she saw an eager-looking stick person wearing a feathered dress.

For the third time, the door swung open and a collective hush fell over the set. A girl a little older than Ivy paused in the doorway, looking every inch a movie star in dark jeans, an off-the-shoulder top and a large moon-shaped pendant necklace. An entourage of people with make-up, refreshments and cell phones waited nervously until she had finished surveying the room and stepped inside. Ivy saw two of the entourage breathe a sigh of relief, almost as if they'd been expecting something bad to happen.

'So far so good,' one of them whispered as they passed Ivy and Sophia's table.

'Jessica Phelps!' Sophia whispered.

People didn't get more famous than Jessica and Jackson. They were at the tippy top of the A-list.

'You know what this means,' Sophia whispered. 'We're not just extras . . . we're extras on the biggest movie of the year!'

Jessica stepped in like she owned the room – and she probably could if she wanted to. She ignored everyone except for Philippe and Jackson, air-kissing them on both cheeks.

'Your hair looks nice,' Jackson said politely.

Jessica smiled. 'Thanks!' She snuggled up to him like he was a teddy bear. Ivy thought she must be trying to stir up some chemistry for the camera, but Jackson just nodded and stepped away slightly.

At least he doesn't respond to every starlet that throws herself at him, Ivy thought approvingly.

'Please, I would like you two to do a run-through before the cameras roll,' Philippe instructed.

'I was just going to suggest that,' Jessica replied.

Jackson and Jessica sat at the fake booth and began to do their lines.

Sophia showed Ivy another napkin. This one had the goateed stick figure and a female stick figure with swirly hair wrestling to control a camera, while a third stick figure lounged back on a chair and watched. The figure with the long hair had Jessica's necklace and the figure lounging in a chair had an 'I Heart Olivia' tattoo on his bicep. Ivy couldn't help it; she burst out laughing in the middle of the rehearsal.

Everyone stopped and stared.

Jessica gasped.

Philippe turned a bright pink. 'What is this?'

he demanded, pointing at them. 'Lillian! What has happened to my silent background artists? These are not silent!'

Lillian came over, caught sight of Sophia's cartoon, stifled a smile and crumpled it behind her back. 'I'm so sorry, Philippe. I hadn't cued them that you were rehearsing.' Ivy felt awful for getting Lillian in trouble.

'No more of that, *merci*!' Philippe said. 'We work!'

Lillian nodded seriously but then turned away and rolled her eyes. She gave Sophia a wink to show she wasn't mad.

Jessica shot an annoyed glance right at Ivy. 'No, we do not work.'

'*Pardon?*' said Philippe. Behind him, two of the film crew exchanged a glance, as if to say: *Here we go again!*

Jessica sniffed. 'I can't work under these

conditions. I have been dragged to this dump of a town where it's cold and I can't get a decent cup of coffee. Then, I suffer through three terrible hairdressers. And you can't even afford good extras. Well, you can now, because I quit!'

Everyone gasped and Jackson looked shocked.

'You c-c-cannot,' Philippe spluttered.

'Clause 38, subsection C: unreasonable conditions,' Jessica retorted.

'Because of coffee?' Philippe shouted, turning even pinker. 'I will sue!'

Jessica turned on her shiny Heather Carter heel. 'My lawyers are much more expensive than yours.'

Her entourage scurried after her and a deathly silence filled the diner.

Charlotte hissed from the next booth over, 'Great job at wrecking everything.'

Ivy felt her mouth turn dry.

Had she and Sophia just ruined the entire film?

Chapter Six

'What do you mean, shut down?' Olivia asked Ivy. Her sister was coming down the steps from the diner into the parking lot, pulling on a warm coat.

'I mean shut down – no female lead equals no filming,' Ivy replied.

Sophia nodded and shivered. Or shivered and nodded. It was so cold out that Olivia couldn't tell which.

It had barely been half an hour since she'd had the fruit cup with Jackson. Since she hadn't found Ivy, she had decided to make her way to the diner to watch some scenes. But when she'd arrived, everyone was hurrying away.

'What happened?' Olivia asked. The girls stood off to the side as other crew members and actors milled around.

'Jessica quit the movie,' Ivy said.

'Never to return,' Sophia added.

Olivia sneaked a peek through the diner windows and saw Jackson listening to his manager, who was shouting at someone sitting in a chair labelled 'Director'. Jackson looked really annoyed.

'Does this mean the movie is over?' Olivia wondered. 'Will Ja– everyone be leaving town?'

'It might be for the best . . .' Ivy said. Something across the parking lot had caught her attention. She craned her neck for a better look and then hurried over to the barriers.

Olivia looked over and realised she was

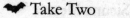

heading towards Brendan and his seven-year-old sister Bethany, who were waving at them from outside the barriers.

As the girls approached, Bethany blurted out, 'Did you get to meet Jackson?' She looked adorable in her black puffy jacket and denim skirt with black leggings.

'Hey, Brendan,' Ivy said. 'Hi, Bethany. Isn't Jackson a bit bunny for you?'

'Duh, Jackson is above all labels,' Bethany replied, flipping her long black hair. 'So did you meet him? Did you?'

Olivia smiled. 'I got to have lunch with him.'

'Eeee!' Bethany squealed, causing several people to jump. 'Are you two going to be on TV together?' she asked more quietly.

Olivia laughed. 'I don't think so.'

'What was he like?' Bethany wanted to know.

'Pretty normal,' Olivia said, remembering

their Count Vira conversation.

'Sounds like you've been having fun,' Brendan said. 'But what about breakfast?'

Right on cue, Ivy's stomach let out a gurgle that a bog monster would envy. 'I completely forgot. You went to the Juice Bar!'

'And came right back here, waiting all day for my beautiful girlfriend with a now gravely cold Breakfast Bun.' Brendan tried to look hurt, but his face was twitching into a smile, even as Ivy was apologising.

'I'm just kidding.' Brendan took a squashed wrapped sandwich from his bag and waggled it in the air. 'When I couldn't find you in the crowd, I went home to get Bethany and may have enjoyed the latest episode of *Night of the Deadly Dead* in the warm.'

Ivy was almost drooling over the sandwich. Olivia laughed as Ivy leaned over the barrier,

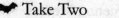

planted a quick kiss on Brendan's cheek and grabbed the packet from his hand. She devoured the bun in three big bites.

Sophia raised one eyebrow. 'Thanks for sharing.'

'Oops,' Ivy said, her mouth full of bacon and red sauce.

'You can have my Count Cocoa Chew.' Bethany held out a candy bar to Sophia, but pulled it away as soon as Sophia reached for it. 'If you get me inside.'

Olivia felt bad. 'But the movie has . . . uh . . . paused for a minute. They've asked everyone to leave.'

'OK, then,' Bethany said. 'Just promise to try to get me something that Jackson has touched.'

'I promise,' Sophia replied, 'to get Olivia to do it for me.'

Bethany narrowed her eyes, looking from

Sophia to Olivia. 'OK, deal.' She handed it over to Sophia.

'How about we –' Brendan began.

'Now,' Bethany interrupted. 'Tell me everything!'

As Ivy explained all about the set, with Sophia butting in and correcting her on the details, Olivia saw Brendan's face falter a little. She hoped he wasn't feeling left out with all the movie excitement. Maybe there would be a way to get him on set tomorrow – that is, if the set was still there tomorrow.

🦇   🦇   🦇

That night, Ivy sat in front of Olivia's computer and clicked on the moon icon to get to the usual all-black screen with three big Gothic letters:

VVV

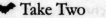

'Good thing they let you have a chip,' Ivy said as she clicked the Vs seven times in the precise pattern that would bring up the password prompt. 'I'd never last two nights in a row without being able to get on to the World Vide Veb.'

Olivia was in her pink pyjamas, sorting through her closet trying to find something to wear for tomorrow. 'I couldn't figure out what was happening when that guy showed up at our house, pretending to be a computer repair man.'

Since her official initiation by the Vampire Round Table, Olivia had been granted all the privileges of the vampire world, including access to the super-secret Vorld Vide Veb, which required a special computer chip to even get to the home page.

'It didn't help that he was wearing a Hawaiian shirt and sandals with socks,' Olivia went on as

Ivy tapped in her user name and password. 'He didn't look a thing like a vamp.'

'It just goes to show that you never can tell,' said Ivy, wondering if Olivia would take the hint. *Think Jackson!* Ivy wanted to shout but Sophia was right. She needed proof.

A riddle popped up and Ivy read it aloud. 'What happens when a vampire gets a cold?'

'Ooh, I know that one,' Olivia said. 'Lots of coffin.'

'Ha, ha.' Ivy typed it in and the MOONLIGHT search screen appeared with its tag line 'Illuminate the darkness,' underneath the entry box.

As soon as Ivy had heard Olivia describe Jackson as 'normal' she'd known Olivia was interested in him, so she had decided to do a little research. If he was on the VVV then Ivy could accidentally leave it up on the screen for her sister to discover. *It would be so much easier if Olivia*

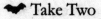

found out for herself that Jackson is anything but normal, Ivy thought as she typed in 'Jackson Caulfield vampire.'

Ivy scanned the screen but the search results didn't list any hints of his possible vampness – only sites like 'Top 50 Bite-able Humans', which put Jackson at number four, and 'Vampires for Jackson for President'.

But just because there was nothing on the VVV, it didn't mean he wasn't a vampire. Lots of movie-star vamps kept it a secret to avoid being typecast as moody brooders by the vamp powers-that-be in Hollywood.

'What do you think of this for me to wear tomorrow?' Olivia held up a green ribbed sweater dress and wide green belt. 'It might be my last chance to see Jackson, so I want to look nice.'

'I'm not sure Jackson is your type,' Ivy said, 'but the belt looks great.'

'Do you mean the way-too-good-looking-and-famous-to-ever-actually-consider-me type?' Olivia sighed and sat down on her bed.

'No!' Ivy didn't want her sister thinking Jackson was out of her league. 'He's way into you.'

'You think so?' Olivia's voice went up an octave.

'It's just he might not be as perfect as you think,' Ivy said, shutting down the VVV and standing up to make her 'bed' for the night.

'He's definitely not perfect,' Olivia said. 'At lunch today, he went all carnivorous on me. I totally expected him to be a veggie, like me, but he had a burger you would have been proud of.'

Carnivorous? Ivy's stomach lurched. *That could count as evidence.* 'Does that mean you don't want to see him any more?' If Olivia was going to give him up anyway, then Ivy could stop her investigations.

'I'd love to keep hanging out with him, as

long as it's not at lunchtime.'

Ivy sighed. She was going to have to get proof
– and that meant going back to the movie set
tomorrow and facing whatever consequences
there might be for Jessica's outburst. She was
clearing the dressing table when there was a
knock at the door.

Ivy whirled around as Olivia said, 'Come in,'
and Mrs Abbott appeared, carrying a tray of warm
milk, some crackers and a bottle of pink digestion
liquid. Good thing it hadn't been a minute later, or
they would have had a tough time explaining why
Olivia's dressing table was on its back.

'You said your tummy was bothering you.' Mrs
Abbott put the tray down on the edge of the bed.

The tummy ache plan from this morning had
worked like a charm, and Ivy had already wolfed
down the roast-beef sandwich they'd bought on
the way home – *mmm*.

Ivy snapped out of the happy memory to say, 'That's so nice of you, Mrs Abbott.' Moms really were awesome.

'I just want to make sure you get a good night's sleep.' Mrs Abbott gave both girls a hug and wished them sweet dreams. 'Olivia, honey, be considerate to our guest and give Ivy the comfy bed tonight.'

Once the door was shut, the sisters burst out giggling.

When they'd recovered, Olivia looked at Ivy and pointed to the bottle of antacid. 'I am *not* drinking that for you.'

🦇   🦇   🦇

Olivia flashed her badge at the security guard.

'Hey, where can I get one of those?' shouted a teen girl from the crowd as Olivia, Ivy, Sophia and Camilla walked through the barriers on to the movie set.

'I want one, too!' called a little girl with a balloon.

Olivia wished she could help. Ivy and Sophia's extras passes were still valid from yesterday, but only her top-level VIP pass allowed her to bring someone in – and it was only one person.

'Sorry!' Olivia called behind her.

As they walked around the parking lot, Olivia could see that the buzz had drained away from the production since yesterday. There were barely any people milling around and anyone who was, looked worried.

'Is this how it's supposed to be?' whispered Camilla, pulling down the hood on her 'Watch the Skies' hoodie.

'Not at all,' Ivy replied.

'There she is.' A snide voice came through the open door of a trailer and Charlotte, followed by a group of extras, stepped out into the cold. 'That zombie girl is the one who ruined the movie for everyone.' Charlotte was pointing right at Ivy.

Ivy glared back at Charlotte.

Olivia had a flashback to a district cheerleading competition at her old school two years ago where two squads had got their ponytails in a twist over an accusation of a stolen stunt.

'It wasn't anybody's fault,' Olivia began, stepping between the two groups. 'The movie is on hold because Jessica wanted to quit.'

'But if it wasn't for your freakish sister –' Charlotte tossed her hair – 'we would all be getting our big chance to break in.'

'Break into the discount store?' Ivy asked.

Charlotte narrowed her eyes. 'No, you ghoul! To Hollywood, California – where people have skin tone?'

'Hey,' Camilla said to Ivy, pointing across the

parking lot. 'Isn't that Steven Spielberg?'

While Charlotte and her crew all strained to see, Camilla hooked her arm through Ivy's and pulled her in the opposite direction. Olivia caught on to what she was doing, grabbed Sophia and followed.

'Losers!' Charlotte shouted after them, once she'd realised they were making their escape.

'If Charlotte ever becomes a celebrity,' Sophia said, looking back over her shoulder, 'I'm moving to Mars.'

'Can I fly the ship?' Camilla asked.

Charlotte being mean didn't matter, but what she'd said made Olivia's heart sink. 'Do you think it really is all over?'

Ivy linked her arm in Olivia's, so they were walking as a foursome. 'I don't know.'

'Olivia!'

Someone ahead of them was waving frantically.

It was Jackson. Her heart did a little cheer of its own.

'I've great news,' he said when the group had gotten closer. He scooped Olivia up in a hug.

Oh my goodness! Olivia thought, stunned but thrilled.

'Come with me!' He grabbed her hand and led them back through the parking lot. 'This is so exciting,' he said. 'And I definitely want you to be a part of it.'

He was tugging her along with such excitement that she felt swept off her feet. She glanced back at her sister to give her an excited grin, but Ivy had a strange look on her face.

What is Jackson talking about? Olivia wanted to know. When they reached the main entrance, Jackson gave her a wink and dropped her hand. He grabbed a megaphone from one of the security guards and hopped up on one of the wide pillars.

'Hello, Franklin Grove!'

The response from the crowd was a mix of squeals, cameras flashing and returned hellos. The movie's crew and other extras were gathering around as well. Something big was about to happen.

'What's going on?' Camilla asked.

Olivia could only shrug and continue to stare up at the world-famous movie star who wanted her to do something that involved a loudspeaker announcement to an entire crowd of his fans.

'If you haven't heard, I'm filming a romantic comedy.'

More shrieking and Olivia saw one girl faint.

'But now I'm missing a leading lady.'

Olivia's tummy did a basket-toss.

'Which means I have to make a very, very special announcement.'

The entire crowd held its breath.

'We had a big meeting last night and decided that the best way to cast a new leading lady is . . .' Jackson gazed around at the upturned faces, grinning. He was making the most of this. Then he shouted into the microphone: 'To find one right here in Franklin Grove!'

Chapter Seven

Once the cheering had quietened, Jackson went on, 'Filming has to start again soon, so the director will be choosing someone quickly. Anyone interested in auditioning should go to the reception trailer just inside the set. We're also making announcements on local radio and counting on you to spread the word to your friends.'

Olivia clapped along with everyone else as he hopped down. The movie hadn't collapsed and Jackson wasn't going to leave! The security guards pulled open the barriers, and a steady stream of girls and a few older women hurried in towards the trailer, casting backwards glances in Jackson's direction.

'I hope you'll try out, Olivia,' Jackson said, back at her side again. 'But even if you don't, at least I'll get to stay in town for a little longer.'

Olivia hoped that he wanted to stay because he wanted to spend more time with her.

Amy Teller strode up, with her cell phone superglued to her ear. 'That's right,' she was saying. 'His name needs to be bigger on the poster – no, bigger than that.' She put her hand over the mouth piece. 'This is going to be *great* publicity,' she said to Jackson. 'I've already called *Inside Hollywood*; they're sending a camera crew straight away.'

She motioned for Jackson to follow her.

'See you on set,' Jackson said to Olivia with a little wave.

When he was gone, Camilla pretended to faint into Olivia's arms. 'He's staying! And he wants you to audition.'

'He was just saying that to be nice.' Olivia forced herself to be sensible. 'He wanted every girl here to audition to have the best chance of finding the right one.'

Camilla shook her head. 'There's enough chemistry between you to fill a text book.'

Olivia rolled her eyes. 'Anyway – it would be ace to get to star in a movie. Are you going to audition?'

Camilla snorted. 'Not a chance. The only way I'll ever be in a movie is inside some green tentacle monster costume.'

Sophia shook her head. 'I'd rather be behind the camera.'

'I'm not exactly what they're looking for,' Ivy dead-panned.

Is Ivy looking a little . . . anxious? Olivia wondered. She couldn't figure out why that would be. Maybe she was still worried about what had happened on set yesterday.

Olivia had already made up her mind about auditioning. 'I'm going to.'

The little group whooped and cheered as she did a double clap, like at the beginning of a cheer, and stepped towards the reception trailer. *This is it. Hollywood, here I come.*

Then she felt a hand on her arm and turned around. Ivy was holding her back.

'What's wrong?' Olivia asked, the excitement fading from her face.

Ivy swallowed. She didn't want her sister getting hurt. *I can't blurt out that Jackson is a vampire without proof,* Ivy thought. But if they ended up starring in a movie together, Olivia could totally end up falling for him. *What should I do?*

141

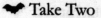

'Ivy?' Olivia was frowning.

At the same time, Ivy couldn't deny that this could be Olivia's big break. The director would have to be a zombie not to see her potential.

Ivy sighed. 'I just wanted to say good luck,' she said, hoping that she'd get some evidence before the role was decided.

Olivia gave her a big hug and scurried off with Camilla to sign up.

'It is now Mission Critical to uncover the truth about Jackson Caulfield,' Ivy said to Sophia as they watched the others leave.

'That he's utterly into your sister?' Sophia replied.

Ivy batted her on the arm. 'I know *that* – it's *because* of that we have to figure out whether or not he's a vampire. Now, I've got a plan.'

Ivy wanted to create some diversion on the other side of the set. That way she could break into the cafeteria truck, steal a chef uniform and pretend to be a caterer so she could find out exactly what food his contract specified.

'All you have to do,' Ivy said, 'is something distracting.' She searched around for inspiration, her glance falling on a loudspeaker. 'Like singing over the megaphone. Or maybe streaking?'

'Um,' Sophia said. 'So many "no's".'

'There you are!' said a voice behind them. 'I was hoping to find you on set somewhere.'

The two girls turned to see Lillian, the second assistant director, who had signed them up to be extras yesterday. Ivy hoped she wasn't going to give them a piece of her mind for what happened yesterday.

'Hi,' Sophia said cautiously.

'Your cartoon was hilarious,' Lillian said.

'Really?' Sophia's voice had gone so high a bat would squeak back. It was pretty cool that a Hollywood director liked her cartoon.

'We thought you'd want to bury us for the Jessica incident,' Ivy said.

'No, but now that you mention it – you can make it up to me. I need some help in the costume trailer.'

'Sure,' Sophia agreed.

As they walked across the parking lot with her, Lillian explained, 'Yesterday was not at all your fault. At first, Jessica tried using car sickness as a medical reason for not doing the movie.'

'But she wouldn't actually be in a car,' Sophia pointed out.

'Exactly. It's just another lame excuse to get out of the shoot.'

Lillian took them inside the huge costume trailer and over to a pile of clothes. 'OK, girls, these need sorting out and hanging up.'

Ivy was more than happy to help with the

costume racks – every kind of top, designer-label jeans, a hundred different belts and sunglasses.

Ivy started helping Sophia with the hats.

'The next excuse from Jessica was an extreme allergy to snow,' Lillian said. 'We responded with understanding and pointed out that would also prevent her from doing anything that required leaving her house for the next three months.'

Ivy mock-gasped. 'But then how would she get on the cover of *Paparazzi Press*?'

Lillian smiled. 'In the end, I'm sure it was because the script is too much about Jackson. You'd think she would have *read* it before signing up. Anyway, now that she's gone, this movie is tabloid paradise – an unknown actress plucked from obscurity, teamed with the biggest teen dream . . . Philippe couldn't have planned it better.'

Ivy realised that she might not need Sophia

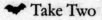

to go streaking after all. Lillian had access to the inner circle with all kinds of information about the people in the movie.

She needed to keep Lillian talking about Jackson. Her mind flashed to the girl in the polka-dot jacket outside and then to Bethany – Jackson fan girls. If Ivy pretended to be a big Jackson fan, she could ask Lillian lots of questions without Lillian wondering why she was asking.

Think perky. Think Mister Smoothie. You can do this! Ivy told herself.

Ivy forced an Olivia-style giggle. 'Whoever they pick for the lead is going to be one lucky girl getting to talk to Jackson all the time.'

Sophia looked at her like she'd grown a second head.

'I mean, he is totally above all labels.' Ivy winced at her own idiocy, hoping that Lillian would buy her act and spill some silver bullets.

Lillian chuckled. 'He certainly isn't at all what you'd expect from his movies.'

In a blood-drinking, coffin-dwelling, fang-filing kind of way? Ivy felt like Lillian was finally going to give her the breakthrough evidence she needed. She clutched the Stetson she was stacking with both hands.

'In a really modest and down-to-earth kind of way,' Lillian finished.

Ivy let out her breath. This guy was completely squeaky clean! He had everybody fooled.

'Except,' Lillian said and Ivy's head whipped back up, 'for the dietary requirement section of his rider.'

Ivy gulped. 'Yes?'

'It's a mile long. For a guy who is so laid back he's almost dead, he sure is particular about his meals.'

Ivy nudged Sophia so hard that she dropped a

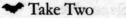

stack of baseball caps, and they scattered all over the floor of the trailer.

'Ivy,' Sophia whispered, as they crouched to pick up the hats. 'Can we *please* stop talking about Jackson?'

'But I'm on the verge –' Ivy started.

'Of getting us escorted off the movie set in handcuffs for harassment,' Sophia finished. She picked up the last hat and gave Lillian a big smile.

Ivy sighed and kept her mouth shut.

'Thanks so much for helping out, girls,' Lillian said. 'Let's see . . . I'm sure I've got . . .' She trailed off as she went rummaging around in a box in the corner. 'Yup! Here it is.' She pulled out a T-shirt that said 'Save the Whales'. 'Jackson wore this last week, during shooting in the studio.'

She handed it to Ivy, with an expectant look, but Ivy couldn't figure out why Lillian would think she wanted a grubby old shirt.

'Wow, Lillian!' Sophia said. 'Thanks so much. Ivy is so excited, she's speechless.' Sophia nudged her hard. 'And I know a little girl who's going to be very jealous.'

Ivy realised that this was primo Jackson memorabilia. Bethany would be utterly thrilled. 'Yeah, thanks!'

After all that, Ivy thought, *I'm still not any closer to proving Jackson's vamp-ness. And I'm running out of time.*

❤ ❤ ❤

'I don't know why any of these people are bothering,' Charlotte said. 'I'm the most qualified for the part; I've already acted with Jackson.'

Olivia bit her lip. That was totally rude, but she didn't want to start an argument in line. It was just her luck to end up right behind Charlotte. 'I think it's exciting that everybody gets a chance,' she said.

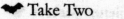

'Humph.' Charlotte rummaged through her bag, pulled out a compact mirror and started applying another layer of mascara.

Katie and Allison were waiting nearby, looking like they'd just come last in a race.

'Aren't you two going to sign up?' Camilla asked them.

'Of course not,' Charlotte answered. 'They're going to be my cheerleaders.'

Katie offered a weak thumbs-up and Allison said, 'Go, Charlotte!' but she wasn't smiling.

Olivia was so glad she wasn't one of Charlotte's closest friends – it didn't seem like much fun.

'And I'm *your* cheerleader,' Camilla said to Olivia. 'But I'm not any good at backflips.'

Olivia giggled and linked her arm in Camilla's.

'Next!' shouted the receptionist sitting at the desk, making Charlotte jump and smudge her mascara under her eye.

'Argh!' Charlotte tried to wipe it away but it just smeared.

'Next!' the woman said even louder. Her hair was in a tight bun and she peered at Charlotte over her reading glasses. 'You! Get over here.'

Charlotte stepped up, one hand covering her eye.

'Name?' the receptionist asked, fingers poised over the keyboard.

Charlotte handed over her extras pass, like it was a golden ticket.

The woman squinted at it. 'Chartreuse Blown?'

Camilla chuckled.

'What? No!' Charlotte snatched the pass back, peered at the details and turned bright red. 'It's Charlotte. Charlotte Brown.'

The woman raised one eyebrow. 'You sure, honey?'

Charlotte blinked furiously. 'Don't be

ridiculous. I know my own name!'

The receptionist smirked and indicated a stack of folders. 'Take one of those and move on.' Charlotte took the top one, clutched it to her chest and stormed past Katie and Allison, who hurried after her.

'Next!' the woman shouted.

That meant Olivia.

❤   ❤   ❤

Ivy didn't want to push it too much with Lillian, but she had to find out the truth about her sister's movie-star crush. She had a plan. She needed Lillian to show them where the food was.

When they had finished with the costumes, Ivy piped up. 'Gosh, I'm starving.'

'Well, we're done here.' Lillian grabbed three pairs of oversized Access sunglasses from their cubby hole, handed a pair each to Ivy and Sophia and said, 'Let's head over to Craft Service.'

All she needed to do was taste one of Jackson's meals and she'd have the proof she needed. If there was any hint of blood, Ivy would be able to tell.

It was still cold outside the costume trailer but sunny, so Ivy was glad of the wicked shades.

'Lillian! Lillian! What is to be done? Have you *seen* the actresses? Oh, *non, non, non!*' How Philippe didn't melt into a puddle of trauma, Ivy didn't know.

'Don't worry.' Lillian tried to calm him down but he was flapping like a black cape in the wind. 'We'll find someone.' She mouthed, 'See you later,' to Ivy and Sophia and led Philippe away.

'What are you up to?' Sophia demanded the moment they were out of earshot.

'I know how I can get proof of Jackson's fanghood,' Ivy said, pulling Sophia towards the big truck labelled 'Craft Service'. 'His mouth!'

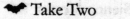

'You're going to call up his dentist?'

'No, I'm going to sneak into wherever they're storing his meals,' Ivy said. 'I don't know exactly where that is, but if it comes down to it, I will sit in the cafeteria and wait until he shows up, so I can know what he's eating.'

Sophia sighed. 'Well, it beats me streaking.'

Ivy hauled herself up into the craft truck and her heart sank. It was a big truck, but there were people everywhere. She guessed that without having anything to film, the crew was just being paid to eat. Every table was full and the line for food was really long.

So much for sneaking around without anyone noticing.

As the line moved slowly forward, it gave Ivy a chance to survey the scene. The rows of chefs were each tending to a different section of the food tables, serving things up on request. Behind them was a man in a smart suit, checking things off on his clipboard, talking to certain people in line and observing. Ivy decided he was the catering manager.

A trim, brown-haired girl, looking stylish and wearing a multi-stranded beaded necklace over a long, loose grey sweater and jeans, caught the manager's attention. Ivy guessed she must be one of the supporting actresses. The manager flipped through his papers, turned to a stainless-steel fridge behind him and took out a tray filled with what looked like raw carrots and celery – and nothing else – and handed it to her.

'Bingo,' Ivy said. 'He's our man and that's our fridge.' The manager walked farther down the tables to talk to one of his staff. 'That must be where they would store Jackson's special meals.'

Ivy and Sophia shuffled forward, past the first table covered with an elaborate salad bar. The people in front were trying to choose between lobster and oysters, so they were forced to wait in front of the second table, one table away from the fridge, just in front of the sandwich selection.

'Do we get to eat this stuff?' Sophia wondered aloud.

A grey-haired man behind the counter piped up: 'Those extras passes get you all access to these culinary delights. We've got something for everyone; just tell old Curtis what you're after.'

'Ooh,' Sophia replied. 'If I could have anything, I'd go for a Philly cheese steak sandwich.'

'Make that two,' Ivy put in.

Curtis rubbed his hands together and beamed. 'Excellent choice, ladies!' He sliced open two white baguettes, put them on a grill behind him and started scooping heaps of shredded beef into a skillet.

Breakfast at Olivia's had been the usual bunny feast, and Ivy felt herself starting to drool.

'How do you plan to get a look in that fridge?' Sophia whispered, snapping Ivy back to the problem at hand.

Ivy noticed that the serving tables were all covered in crisp white tablecloths. If she could get under this table, she could crawl to the next table, take a quick peek in the fridge and crawl back without being seen.

'Oh look,' Ivy said deliberately. 'My shoelace has come undone.' She knelt down and pretended to tie her bootlace, while pushing up the tablecloth. There was nothing stored under the table, and no one was paying any attention to her, so she lifted the cloth up higher, nudged forward and ducked.

'Ow!' Ivy clanged her head against hard metal, sending a jolt through the plates and bowls of food above her. It felt like she'd been smacked on the forehead by a frying pan.

The stylish brown-haired girl and a group of camera men turned to stare. Ivy staggered to her feet, trying to look dignified.

'She's OK!' Sophia announced and people turned back to their meals.

'Ow.' Ivy rubbed her forehead. 'Must be a low shelf.'

Curtis came back with two steaming beef sandwiches dripping with cheese and onions. The smell of the food made her head injury feel a little better.

Hoping for an opportunity to present itself, Ivy and Sophia spent ages at every food table.

People behind started overtaking them. But eventually, they were at the end of the tables and out of options. Ivy gulped.

'I'll cover you,' Sophia whispered. She put down her tray, held up her camera and said to the manager, 'Hi! I'm making a kind of yearbook scrapbook of the making of this movie. Can I take your picture?'

The manager beamed. 'Sure!' He put his arm around the chef he was talking to, who struck a goofy grin, while Sophia snapped away.

Ivy knew this was her last chance. She clutched her tray, darted behind Sophia and moved to go around the photo shoot, but at the same time the manager stepped backwards to call for another chef to join the photo.

The manager banged right into Ivy, sending her tray full of food and his clipboard flying into the air. He managed to catch her sandwich but everything else ended up on the floor, with his clipboard bursting open smack in the middle of the mess of sushi, satsuma and shrimp. Ivy could hear Sophia's camera still clicking away.

Oh my darkness, Ivy thought. *I want to disappear.*

But as Ivy was sprawled among the debris, she caught sight of one of the sheets of paper. It was labelled 'Dietary Requirements' and had a long list of codes on one side with food allergies on the other.

She didn't get a long look before the manager picked them up, but it was long enough to see right at the top in bold and underlined: 'J-02: ABSOLUTELY NO GARLIC'.

Bingo.

Chapter Eight

'Ladies, please!' Philippe cried.

Jackson had just walked into the Meat & Greet and now not a single one of the hopeful actresses was paying any attention to what Philippe was saying.

Including Olivia.

The production crew had cleared all the furniture out of the dining section of the diner and brought in folding chairs for everyone to sit on.

'Ladies, we must begin the screen tests!' Philippe looked like he was ready to explode from all the stress. 'Now that she-who-must-not-be-named has done what-must-not-be-said, every minute is costing!'

Philippe paced, stopping every few steps to wave his hands and emphasise his words as he explained the rules. 'OK, each candidate gets one chance in front of the camera to impress me. Those who do, come back for a reading with Jackson this afternoon. Those who don't should be ashamed for wasting my time. That is all.'

Olivia gulped. *Not much of a pep talk*, she thought.

The first audition was a red-headed girl at least three years younger than Olivia, who looked like she might be turning a little bit green.

'Look into the camera,' Philippe barked.

The girl held her hands together, almost like she was praying, and looked at the camera. Olivia could see her trembling. *Poor thing*, she thought.

Everyone here really wants the part.

A woman with frizzy hair and a thick New York accent spoke a little softer. 'Tell us your name and age, please.'

But the girl was so camera-struck that she couldn't get the words out. It made Olivia feel even more nervous. *What if I can't speak in front of the camera either?* she wondered.

The auditionee shook her head and the woman came over, put her arm around her and led her outside.

Philippe had no sympathy. 'Next!' he shouted, clearly making a big line through the poor girl's name on his list.

An older blonde girl wearing a green woolly hat and big hoop earrings stood up, looking more confident.

'Now we will see into your soul,' Philippe pronounced. 'The soul of the actress!'

He began firing questions at the girl. 'When did you last laugh? What do you think of frogs? What if the earth was flat?'

The girl did her best to come up with answers, while Philippe scribbled furiously, but some of the questions were totally bizarre. When she'd finished, Philippe nodded, seemingly satisfied.

One by one, girls stood in front of the camera, having to impersonate the president, talk about their pet hamster or describe how they would make a peanut-butter-and-jelly sandwich. Charlotte got a question about her hobbies and she didn't hesitate to tell everyone about being the captain of the cheerleading squad. She happily demonstrated a cheer – the one Olivia wrote last semester.

When they were more than halfway through the people waiting, Philippe called for Olivia.

'I know I'm not supposed to say "good

luck"',' Camilla said. 'So break a tentacle.'

'Thanks,' Olivia replied and stepped in front of the camera. There were lights rigged up on big metal frames and the man with the huge headphones was dangling a microphone over her head.

She felt everyone watching her, waiting to see what she would say. The big black camera was pointing right at her and she wished Ivy could have been here for support. But this was her chance and she was going to give it her best.

'What is your favourite colour and why?'

That was easy. Olivia gave a big smile. 'My favourite colour is pink. And I think it's because when I was four, my mom gave me a frilly pink parasol with my name embroidered on it.'

'What is your darkest secret?'

That I know vampires are real, Olivia thought. She paused for a second and then said, 'I'm

165

adopted. Not that it's a *dark* secret, or anything. But I haven't met most of my biological family.' She didn't want anyone to get suspicious that there was anything unusual about her family. 'But I'd like my biological dad to introduce me to them some day.'

'Sing me a song,' Philippe demanded.

Olivia resisted the urge to break into 'The Right One' and decided to go with 'Double Trouble'. She knew her voice wasn't too bad, and it made it even better when she saw Jackson nodding along.

'Tell us a joke.'

She tried not to let any panic show on her face . . . a joke, a joke. It was so hard to just come up with one on demand. 'Got one!' she said. It wasn't outrageous, just one that always made her chuckle. 'Why don't seagulls fly over the bay?'

She paused and waited for Philippe to respond.

He tapped his pencil on his pad, clearly thinking.
'I don't know. Why not?'

'Because then, they'd be bagels.'

Olivia heard a little snort from behind the camera and saw that the cameraman had laughed at her joke. She stole a quick glance around and everyone watching seemed to be enjoying themselves. *That must be good!* she thought.

'One last question, please,' Philippe said, narrowing his eyes. She sensed he was going to ask a tough one to try to test her.

'What is the best thing that has ever happened to you?'

Olivia didn't hesitate. 'My sister. Even though we're really different from each other, she's my best friend.'

'Thank you very much –' Philippe checked his notes – 'Olivia.'

She stepped out from the glare of the lights

and felt a rush of adrenaline, like she'd just landed a triple handspring. She definitely wanted to do that again, make people laugh and smile. Maybe she had a chance?

Camilla gave her a huge hug and she sat back down in her seat, in a happy daze. 'I think Jackson is smiling at you,' Camilla said.

Olivia snapped her head up to see Jackson *was* smiling at her.

Charlotte was sitting just behind her. 'I think he's smiling at *me*,' she said.

But when he made a thumbs-up sign, Olivia knew he was telling her she'd done well.

Charlotte humphed and snapped at Katie to help fluff her hair again.

Olivia watched the next audition, daring to hope that she had done enough to get through to the read-through. When the screen tests were finally over, Philippe consulted his clipboard.

'We have six candidates going through to the reading later this afternoon. If I read your name, please see Lillian, our second assistant director, for the scripts you will need to learn.'

The frizzy-haired woman held up a stack of folders.

Olivia took a deep breath and Camilla squeezed her hand.

'Evie Dawson, Jane Noble, Rachel Bowden, Lauren Kaler —' Each name was punctuated by a little squeal from the lucky girl and a thud in Olivia's heart. There were only two names left. 'Olivia Abbott and Charlotte Brown.'

Olivia clapped and Camilla did a little happy dance, but Charlotte tossed her hair. 'Obviously, *I* made it through,' she said and immediately started pushing through the crowd of disappointed girls that didn't get called, to get her folder.

'I just want to say,' Jackson stood next to

Philippe and addressed the unsuccessful hopefuls, 'that you all did a fantastic job. I especially liked hearing about Harry the Hamster and how to plant sunflowers.' The girls who'd given those answers beamed at the recognition. 'And just because you didn't get through doesn't mean you should give up. If you want to be an actor, keep trying. That's how I got to be where I am.'

He knows just what to say to make everyone feel better, Olivia thought, still buzzing with excitement that she'd been one of the lucky ones.

Olivia couldn't deny it. Jackson was perfect boyfriend material.

❤   ❤   ❤

Sophia refused to leave the craft service truck until they'd eaten their steak sandwiches, but Ivy was itching to get to Olivia.

I've got my proof, Ivy thought. *Now I can say something before Olivia gets in too deep!*

'Will you admit it now?' Ivy asked Sophia as they finally set off.

Sophia sighed. 'It looks like you were right.'

'Ha!' Ivy said. 'And now I've got to warn Olivia.'

'Warn Olivia about what?' Charlotte Brown had stopped right in front of them, flanked by Katie and Allison.

'Uh.' Ivy had to come up with something convincing but uninformative – and quick! 'Warn her about . . . the competition! I heard there's a girl trying out who's been in some TV commercials.'

Charlotte rolled her eyes. 'That doesn't matter. Philippe has already announced those of us who got through – and, even though Olivia made it, I'm practically under contract already.'

Ivy felt a rush of pride that her sister had made it through, but was now doubly determined to find her and tell her what she'd learned about

Jackson. She shouldn't go giving her heart away without knowing who she was giving it to. She threw an urgent look at Sophia.

'Well,' Ivy said. 'Watch out for those other auditionees. They'll do anything for the job.'

Charlotte put her hands on her hips. 'Like they'd get past me.'

'By the way.' Ivy tried to sound casual. 'Have you seen Olivia?'

'She said she wanted to hang around in the diner more,' Charlotte said.

Ivy thanked her and headed across the parking lot to the Meat & Greet, which was completely surrounded by people. It looked like every unsuccessful budding actress was waiting to catch another glimpse of Jackson.

'I can't see Olivia,' Ivy said to Sophia.

Sophia was a few inches taller and stood on her tiptoes to look over the crowd. 'Maybe we should try to push our way through to the diner?'

Ivy nodded. She had to find her sister, right away.

🦇　　　🦇　　　🦇

Olivia and Camilla were tucked away in a corner of the reception trailer, as far from the chaos of the diner as they could get. Any other time, she would have waited for Jackson with the others but Olivia wanted to get to work memorising her lines in peace.

The lines were from the opening scene and were supposed to make Jackson's character, Chase, fall in love with Mia. The thought of doing a romantic scene with Jackson made Olivia feel a little shy, but she was just going to have to put all that to one side and be professional.

'Ready?' Camilla said.

'Let's do it,' Olivia replied.

173

She started the scene by reaching for a box of tissues on the windowsill, pretending it was the last half-shell of coconut juice at a Hawaiian buffet. Camilla, playing Jackson's part, did the same and bumped into her.

Camilla read, 'Chase looks into Mia's eyes and what he sees stops him in his tracks.' She dropped her jaw and slapped her hands on either side of her mouth.

'Ha, ha,' Olivia replied, but she stayed in character and kept going with the lines.

'Chase grabs a coconut from the fruit display in one hand and Mia's hand in the other and pulls her to the beach,' read Camilla. She grabbed the tissues and hit the box with a nearby can of drink. 'Chase tries to smash open the coconut with a rock. "I'm going to open it for you," he says.' Camilla said Chase's lines in a deep, very unconvincing man's voice.

'Maybe if you were wearing a grass skirt,' Olivia/Mia teased.

'Maybe if I'd just taken that last coconut drink, I wouldn't be humiliating myself,' was Camilla/Chase's reply.

'I'm glad you didn't.' Olivia knew this was supposed to be the really romantic bit where she admits a little that she likes him. 'Because watching you try to crack that nut is the funniest thing I've seen this trip.'

'So you think that you could do better?' Camilla/Chase challenged.

The script had Mia take the rock from Chase. Olivia had never opened a coconut before but the script made it pretty clear. 'You see these three indents here?' She pointed at two of the letters on the can. 'The Polynesians say that these three indents are the face of the coconut. These two are the eyes and this is the mouth. The mouth is the weakest point.'

Olivia pretended to strike the coconut and get it open. Then she was supposed to smile the most beautiful smile Chase has ever seen. To make herself do this just right she thought of the moment when Jackson grabbed her hand before the big announcement about the auditions.

'You know, you're really good at this,' Camilla said, dropping the silly manly voice. 'When you said those lines, you became this whole new character. It was you, but you were different – and I really believed what you were saying.'

'Thanks, Camilla.'

'You should definitely be an actress.'

Olivia was always comfortable entertaining people when she was cheering, and she had to be super-careful about the vampire secret; maybe acting was just another form of all that? And lately, she could find plenty of inspiration for romance. 'Maybe today will be my big break,' she said.

'But remember that if Philippe is stupid enough to give the part to someone else, it doesn't mean you aren't good,' Camilla countered.

Charlotte Brown stepped into the reception trailer. 'What are you doing here?' Charlotte said to Olivia. For once, she was without Katie and Allison.

'Duh,' Camilla retorted. 'Olivia made the callbacks, too.'

Charlotte waved her hand like Camilla was a second-squad cheerleader. 'It's just that I'm surprised you're still here practising.'

'What do you mean?' Olivia asked.

'I thought you'd be with Ivy,' Charlotte replied. 'She looked really upset, arguing on the phone with someone.' Charlotte leaned in and lowered her voice. 'Looks like Dracula and

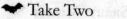 Take Two

Dracu-less are on the out and out.'

Olivia realised with a start that they had forgotten Brendan again this morning. She felt terrible if he and Ivy were fighting, especially because they kept coming to the set for Olivia. *This is my fault*, she thought. She had to find Ivy. 'Where is she?'

Charlotte shrugged. 'Brewing up curses in her cauldron?'

'Charlotte,' Olivia warned, her face settling into one of Ivy's death stares. Captain or no captain, if Ivy was upset, there was no time for diplomacy. 'Where is she?'

'OK, OK.' Charlotte tossed her hair. 'She told the other spook that she was going to the mall to get away from everything.'

Olivia started packing up her stuff, folding the script into her purse. 'I've got to get to the mall.'

'But what about the audition? The read-through?' Camilla asked. 'Can't you just call her?'

'This is more important. Ivy and Brendan never fight. It must be huge,' Olivia said. They were the perfect couple and she wasn't going to let something come between them. She would help fix it, help explain to Brendan. 'She'll need someone with her, not a voice on the phone.'

Ivy came before the audition. Olivia had to go.

Chapter Nine

Looking for Olivia among this crowd of Jackson super-fans was like looking for a real vampire on Halloween.

Ivy had figured out eventually that Charlotte had lied about Olivia being in the diner. When Ivy and Sophia managed to force their way in, one of the production crew said all the finalists had left right after the announcement.

One point to Charlotte.

Now, Sophia was off talking to Lillian and resting her feet, while Ivy wandered in circles. It had been almost two hours since she'd found the 'garlic clause' as she was now referring to it, and she still hadn't been able to tell Olivia the truth about Jackson.

Ivy sat down to rest on one of the parking plinths, her legs crossed in front of her.

Ivy's phone rang from inside her bag. Hoping it was Olivia, she started digging for it, pulling out her key chain, her notebook and the packet of O-Neg flavoured lollipops that Brendan had given her before Christmas. She found her phone on the sixth ring.

'Thank the darkness!' Ivy said.

'I'm so sorry,' Olivia blurted. 'It's all my fault, but we can fix it. I'll help.'

Ivy was a little confused; she wasn't *that* upset about not being able to find Olivia. 'Fix it? There's nothing to fix. I just need to talk to you.'

'I know,' Olivia said. 'That's why I'm here –

and there *is* something to fix. You can't give up so easily.'

'Give up?' Ivy was getting really confused.

'Love is worth fighting for,' Olivia said.

'Um, OK,' Ivy replied. She started to think that maybe Olivia already knew. Maybe Jackson had broken the First Law of the Night and told her. And maybe that meant that Olivia had gotten over it and would be happy with a vampire boyfriend after all.

'Now tell me where you are,' Olivia instructed.

'I'm right in the middle, near the fake palm trees,' Ivy said.

'Is that by the pet store?'

'No,' Ivy replied, thinking Olivia must be joking. The closest thing to a pet store on set was the make-up trailer where Spencer groomed and fluffed his actors like poodles. Ivy decided to play along. 'It's next to the cake shop.'

Olivia didn't respond for a moment. 'There's a cake shop in the mall?'

Now Ivy was completely baffled. 'The mall?'

'Yes, the mall,' Olivia said. 'The mall where you are.'

'I'm not at the mall,' Ivy said slowly. 'I'm on set where *you* are supposed to be.'

'But –' Olivia started. 'But . . . but . . .'

There was a terrible pause as Ivy couldn't figure out what to say.

Olivia finally broke the silence. 'You're not at the mall.'

'Why in the name of all that is gory would I go to the mall now? And why would you?'

Olivia sighed. 'Charlotte Brown.'

Olivia explained what Charlotte had told her, and the truth sunk in.

'It's true that Brendan might be feeling a little left out, but we didn't fight,' Ivy said.

'I haven't spoken to him today.'

Two points to Charlotte, Ivy thought. *Or maybe more like ten.*

'She was just trying to get me off set, so I'd miss the callbacks,' Olivia said and Ivy could hear her start to get breathless as she hurried through the mall. 'And it looks like she succeeded!'

Ivy looked down at her spooky pumpkin watch. 'You'll never get back in time.'

'I know!' Olivia said quietly. She sniffled. 'It wasn't just Jackson; it was the part. I really thought I had a chance.'

Grrr, Ivy thought. *Arg.* She wanted to hang Charlotte up by her fake designer-label boots. *She is so devious!*

'Now there really is something to fix,' Ivy said, looking around at the film people passing by, to see if there was someone she could tell. 'We're not going to let Charlotte win. I'll go and stall them.' She jumped up from the plinth.

'You couldn't stall Philippe with an apocalypse,' Olivia replied. 'But there is something we could do.'

Olivia's tone of voice made Ivy brace herself for what was coming.

'Even though I'm not on set, there happens to be someone who looks just like me there.'

Ivy knew what Olivia meant. 'You mean switch?'

'It's the only way,' Olivia said. 'You can be me for the callbacks, at least until I get there. Camilla is still on set; she's got my copy of the script.'

Ivy gulped. 'Um . . .'

She knew her sister wanted this role – and that she'd be perfect for it – but learning lines and going in front of the camera on her behalf could be a disaster. *Bigger than Olivia not showing up at all?* she thought. Maybe, if Ivy got the part and got to spend time with Jackson, she could figure out once and for all whether he was a vampire.

'Jackson doesn't know we're twins, I don't think. I've never told him. And you've fooled everyone else before.' Olivia's voice got quiet. 'Please?'

'OK, I'll do it.' Ivy felt a little flush of panic saying it but knew her sister would go to the same lengths for her.

Olivia squealed down the phone and Ivy had to hold it away from her ear. When she put it back, Olivia was saying, 'OK, go get bunny-fied. I'm leaving right now and will be there as soon as I possibly can. Love you, sis.'

'Love you, too.' But Ivy felt like a gravestone was on her shoulders. How was she going to find Camilla, learn lines and pink up in the next half an hour plus impress a highly strung director and teen-dream movie star?

It would take superpowers – ones she didn't have!

I'll just have to do my best and not let Olivia down, Ivy decided.

🦇   🦇   🦇

Ten minutes later, Camilla was barking out lines of perky, romantic dialogue while Ivy smeared off her dark eyeliner with make-up remover. Sophia was outside standing guard. They had decided to sneak into the make-up trailer first because she couldn't go to get her Mia costume looking Goth-gorgeous or they would never believe she was Olivia.

'I'm going to open it for you,' said Camilla in a voice that made Ivy think of the giant from *Jack and the Beanstalk.*

Which didn't help her remember her lines. 'Um.' Ivy kept getting confused about the exact wording. 'Something something grass skirt?'

She wiped her face with a towel and started to rummage through the colours of spray tan in the box in front of her.

'Ivy!' Camilla whacked Ivy on the arm with the script. 'It's "Maybe if you were wearing a grass skirt". Olivia had this nailed in the first five minutes.'

'Sorry,' Ivy said, choosing the Santa Monica that Spencer had used the day before. 'I'm not cut out for this acting thing. But since Olivia clearly is, I've got to at least try for her.'

Camilla sighed. 'OK. Here's the plan: if you forget a line during the reading you're just going to have to improv.'

'What's that?' Ivy finished dabbing her face with fake tan and waved her hands in front of her cheeks to help it dry faster.

'Improvise. Be spontaneous. In all the Gary Spellman movies, the actors become one with their alien characters and are so fluent in Fragmala, that they just make up the dialogue as they go along. It's much more authentic that way.'

Camilla really knows her alien stuff, Ivy thought.

'OK, improv. Got it.' She opened Spencer's eye-shadow box and gasped. There were eight trays of three rows each, with dozens of shades of every possible colour. How could she pick? She would just have to guess at what Mia would choose – or what *Olivia* as Mia would choose. She grabbed an eye brush and reached for the light purples.

The door banged open, making both girls jump.

Busted, Ivy thought.

'No, no, no!' said Spencer.

Sophia followed, mouthing, 'Sorry!'

'Please forgive me, Spencer,' Ivy said, as the make-up artist stormed over. Camilla scooted around to the opposite side of the chair. 'I've got a callback in fifteen minutes –'

'And that is why you should not be doing this alone!' Spencer plucked the eye brush from Ivy's hand and tossed it across the room. 'Not purple, darling. Not at all. You must leave the make-up to the professionals.'

Ivy smiled. He wasn't going to throw them out – he was going to help. 'You're an angel,' Ivy declared.

'I heard one of my extras got in. I'm so glad it was you!' Spencer clapped his hands really quickly. 'Now, you,' he said to Camilla. 'Start from the top.'

Camilla started running through the scene, while Spencer worked his magic on Ivy's face.

Ivy didn't have any problems in the costume trailer convincing people she was Olivia, but she was seriously uncomfortable in the short floral sundress they'd given her to wear. Firstly, it was freezing outside, so sundress did not equal fun. Secondly, Hawaiian print was just about as humiliating as it could get. She had forced Sophia to promise not to take a single photo.

'It's for Olivia,' Ivy muttered to herself through clenched teeth as she pushed open the door to the diner where they were doing the read-through. Sophia and Camilla were right behind her.

Ivy had always liked Camilla, but today she had learned what a good friend she really was. Camilla had come up with a set of hand-signal codes to help prompt Ivy if she forgot her lines.

I just have to remember what they mean, Ivy thought wryly.

Ivy took a deep breath, tossed her hair in an Olivia-like fashion and strode over to the other girls who were auditioning. Her heart sank when she saw a familiar, annoying figure absorbed in instructing the lighting man.

Not only was she going to have to act like Olivia in front of a camera, she was going to have to fool Charlotte Brown, too.

When Charlotte realised 'Olivia' wasn't at the mall, her face clouded over for a moment. 'Olivia!' She hurried over. 'Whew! I'm so glad you made it back in time.'

Philippe stormed in, with a look of grim determination. Jackson and his manager followed, smiling and chatting.

Jackson saw Ivy, started to smile and then faltered.

He knows, Ivy thought.

But he finished the smile, looking a little puzzled, and came over. 'Hey, Olivia, you look great!'

'Really?' Ivy mumbled.

Charlotte interrupted. 'Hi, Jackson.' She grabbed his arm. 'I'm so looking forward to working with you.'

He patted Charlotte's hand like he would a grandmother's. 'Thank you.' But he didn't take his eyes off Ivy. 'Could I talk to you in private for a minute, Olivia?'

Ivy was torn between the satisfaction of annoying Charlotte and the fear of getting caught. She shot a look over to Camilla and Sophia, who shrugged. There was nothing she could do to get out of it. She let Jackson lead her to a quiet corner of the diner.

Jackson sat down in one of the booths and ran his fingers through his hair. 'Um, Olivia,' he began. He was staring at her intently.

He knows, Ivy thought. *I'm busted.*

'Jackson!' Amy, his manager, called over, interrupting.

'Later,' Jackson called back firmly.

Ivy saw Amy's mouth snap shut in surprise.

Maybe I can beg him to let me audition anyway, Ivy hoped. *Maybe he'll understand if I explain what happened?*

'I know it seems impossible and complicated,' he said.

You're telling me, Ivy thought.

'But there's something going on here.'

'I know –' she started, but he held up his hand.

'Just let me say this, or I might never get it out.' He crumpled up and smoothed out a napkin.

Ivy gulped back her confession. If the truth was going to come out, it didn't really matter who said it.

'I've never met anyone like you.' His eyes were searching hers. 'You are fun and sweet and smart and beautiful.'

Ivy felt like she was being hit by a ton of

coffins. He hadn't figured out that she was Olivia's twin; he was asking Olivia out!

'I'd really like to see you. I mean off-set. You know? No matter how the audition goes. I know I live far away and I might be leaving town soon. But maybe we could go for lunch somewhere?'

Ivy could see from the state of the napkin that he was really nervous. She decided, if he wasn't a vampire, she would definitely approve of him for her sister.

'Uh . . .' Ivy knew 'Really' wouldn't cut it in this situation. And she couldn't ruin this for Olivia, whether he was a vampire or not. Jackson obviously really liked her and she had to let Olivia answer for herself. 'Look,' she said. 'This might sound weird, but could you ask me again later?'

Jackson paused in his napkin shredding and looked confused. 'Later?'

Ivy chose her words carefully. 'It's not that

. . . I . . . wouldn't want to; it's just that I'm not really . . . myself . . . at the moment. But after the audition, everything will be back to normal.' Ivy desperately hoped that was true. 'So ask me again – just like you did then – later. Using those exact words.'

'Uh . . .' It was clear Jackson didn't know how to respond.

'I, um . . .' Ivy had to come up with some excuse besides, *I'm only impersonating the person you want to be dating, so you're asking the wrong girl.* 'I just want to get through the audition.'

Jackson nodded. 'I understand. Keep it professional. I can respect that.'

To her relief Jackson didn't look like he thought she was one witch short of a coven.

He nodded slowly. 'OK. Maybe I'll ask you again later.'

'Thank you.' She'd got away with it.

'Jackson!' Philippe called from across the set. 'We're ready for you.'

'Good luck in your audition,' Jackson said as he slid out of the booth. 'Even if you don't want to go out with me, I still hope you get the part.'

I hope Olivia does, too, Ivy thought. 'Thanks.'

The first girl to audition was a blonde with big hoop earrings, and she got Phillipe to smile. Even Charlotte looked good on the TV screens they'd set up; she didn't mess up a single line.

'There is no way I can compete with these girls,' Ivy whispered to Sophia, who squeezed her hand.

Maybe Ivy could stall? Maybe Olivia would make it back in time? Maybe the cameras would break or Philippe would have a desperate urge for a croissant and postpone the auditions. But as each girl finished going through the lines with Jackson, Ivy knew it was another nail in her coffin.

'Olivia Abbott,' Philippe called.

Ivy's stomach flipped over.

Camilla held up two sets of crossed fingers and Jackson gave her a warm smile. Ivy stepped on to the tiny x made out of tape on the floor.

Ivy's mouth went dry and her glance darted from the camera to Jackson to a frowning Philippe and then stuck on the floor. She felt her pulse pounding.

Jackson leaned over. 'You're gonna do great. Relax!'

Ivy's face flushed. She instructed herself not to faint.

'And . . . *action!*' shouted Philippe.

Ivy stared at the camera and couldn't move. Everyone was silent. Jackson whispered, 'It's your line.'

'Oh. Um,' Ivy said. 'You can have the coconut. You got here first.' It came out quiet and very high-pitched.

'Louder,' barked Philippe from behind the camera. 'The mic can't pick that up.'

Ivy lifted her head. She had to project, like Olivia made her to when they switched for cheerleader tryouts. 'You got here first!' she shouted, making Jackson wince and take a step back. The microphone man yanked his earphones away from his ears.

Oops.

'Maybe somewhere in between,' Jackson whispered.

They finally stumbled past the first few lines, until they came to the part that Ivy always got wrong – the grass skirt.

She looked past the camera to Camilla who was doing a little hula dance but Ivy's mind went blank. She couldn't think of anything other than the words 'grass skirt' and Camilla's dancing wasn't helping. Then she remembered the whole improvising idea.

Ivy starting doing a hula dance, too, waggling her hands and humming some Hawaiian-style music. She felt ridiculous but it was better than standing there like a mummy. She saw Camilla bury her face in her hands.

'What are you doing?' Jackson said, staying in character but clearly asking her why she was acting like a lunatic.

'I'm doing a dance to the coconut gods.'

Jackson chuckled.

'No, no, no!' Philippe interrupted. 'You must stay on script. We begin again, from before the silly dancing. Take two!'

'I thought it was funny,' Jackson replied.

Ivy still didn't know what the next line was. Everything was moving in slow motion. Philippe was leaning forward. Charlotte was sneering and Jackson was smiling with encouragement. She had approximately ten seconds to figure out the next line.

Luckily, there was a shout from outside and several flashes. There were people and cameras pressed up against the diner windows, with security guards trying to pull them away.

'What is this?!' Philippe started flapping. 'Who called the media?'

Jackson's manager shushed him. 'I called them! This is publicity that money can't buy,' Amy said. 'It's *Inside Hollywood*! Girls, follow me.' She strode to the door. 'I'm so glad you could make it,' she called to the jostling crowd and the security guards backed off. 'Gather round! I'm Amy Teller, Jackson's representative, and will be happy to answer any questions before we do the photo op with Jackson and the girls.'

'But we are already behind the schedule,' Philippe spluttered.

'Do you want to be the lead story on tonight's entertainment news?' Amy demanded, which shut Philippe up.

The crowd shouted out questions and Ivy breathed a sigh of relief. Her audition was forgotten for the moment. She slipped away to find Sophia and Camilla and go over her lines again.

They were sitting up at the diner's bar watching the chaos outside.

'Let me see the script!' Ivy said.

Camilla handed it over and Ivy flipped it open.

Just then, she felt something hit her ear. She looked down at the counter and saw a peanut.

Then another one clonked her forehead.

'Hey!' she said, looking in the direction of the kitchen area, where the miniature missiles must have come from.

A third one arced through the serving window and landed on Camilla's hand.

'What's going on?' Ivy wondered aloud. Maybe it was another of Charlotte's sabotage plans? If Olivia smelt of peanuts and salt, then Philippe would think she was a compulsive snacker and not choose her?

But then she saw a hand waving through the serving window, and a face popped up. Olivia!

Ivy's heart leaped. Her cheerleader in shining armour! Now was her chance to stop this train wreck.

'I'll cover you while you jump over the counter,' Camilla whispered. She hopped off her stool and started questioning Philippe about his previous movies. Everyone else was focused on the cameras outside.

Ivy pushed herself up on to the counter, swung her legs round and then dropped down to the ground. She crawled along, past the shelves of fountain glasses, empty fries baskets stacked neatly and rows of ketchup, salt and pepper shakers, and maple syrup. The door to the kitchen was a swinging one, so she pushed it open tentatively and slipped inside.

'Olivia?' she whispered as loud as she dared.

'Ivy!' came the reply.

Ivy shuffled in the direction of the voice and found Olivia hiding by the fryer.

'You made it!' Ivy gave Olivia a huge hug.

'Just in time for the dance to the coconut gods,' Olivia said.

'Sorry about that,' Ivy said. 'But you're here now, so let's switch.'

Ivy slipped on the green sweater dress.

'I love this Hawaiian print,' Olivia said, admiring the sundress.

Ivy pushed Olivia towards the kitchen door. 'I think you're going to have to be in some photos before your audition starts again. See if you can step in front of Charlotte!'

'Thanks, sis. I owe you one.'

'No, we owe *Charlotte* one for all this,' Ivy replied. 'Now go out there and get that part!'

Olivia couldn't stop smiling. She was having so much fun reading through the lines with Jackson. They'd gotten through the coconut part and were at the scene where he was chasing her through the surf under the moonlight. Olivia could imagine how romantic that would look on screen.

'Mia, I –' Jackson said, holding her arm.

He drew her close. Olivia held her breath. All the cameras and crew and lights seemed to disappear. She could imagine being on a beach with Jackson. She looked up at him, his blue eyes sparkling. Their faces were so close Olivia was having trouble swallowing. She knew he was supposed to say the rest of his line, so why didn't he? Was he going to kiss her?

Olivia couldn't deny it any more. Being near Jackson made her happier than tofu salads. Her heart raced.

'Mia, I wish you didn't have to leave.'

'Me, too,' Olivia whispered. She felt herself rising on to her tiptoes, ever so slightly, closing her eyes, then . . .

'CUT!' shouted Philippe and the spell was broken.

Olivia sank back on to her heels. She blinked in the glare of the lights and saw all the camera crew staring.

'Good, good, yes.' Philippe clapped. 'Thank you all, ladies. We will think on this, watch these tapes and announce our decision tomorrow.'

Olivia sat down on one of the stools, feeling amazed by the moment she'd just had with

Jackson and wondering if she'd done enough to get the part.

'It's almost like you were a different person that second time,' Jackson said, sitting down next to her and swivelling in semi-circles. 'You were so good!'

All Olivia could do was smile.

Jackson paused. 'Is now later?'

'What?' Olivia had no idea what he meant.

'Does now count as later? Can I ask you again?'

Olivia realised this must be something that happened when she was switched with Ivy. 'Sure, you can ask me now.'

'Well, like I said, I've never met anyone like you.'

Olivia's heart started to pound. *Is what I think is about to happen actually happening?*

'You are smart and beautiful and a really good actress.'

Olivia held her breath. *Oh my pompoms, it* is

happening! she realised. Her mouth went dry.

'Could we hang out off-set, away from all the craziness? Just you and me?'

Olivia gulped. Her movie-star crush was asking her out! Underneath all the Hollywood glamour, he was a normal guy. The kind of normal guy she would love as a boyfriend. It wasn't like he was a vampire or anything. *If he wants to take me out, I'm going to let him*, she decided.

'Yes,' she said.

'Yes?' Jackson replied. 'Yes!' He got so excited that he spun all the way round in his chair.

'Jackson!' Amy stopped right in front of them, one hand on her hip. '*Inside Hollywood* wants to interview you on camera.'

'Sorry to rush off. I'll call you later,' he said to Olivia and hurried away.

Olivia was stunned.

Camilla came up to her. 'From the grin on

your face, something big just happened.'

Olivia nodded. 'He asked me out!' This was major. She had to tell Ivy. She had to tell everyone! No, she shouldn't tell people. 'I'm calm,' she said aloud. 'I'm not freaking out.' But she guessed she was smiling like an idiot.

'I would be freaking out,' Camilla admitted.

'OK, I am.' Olivia needed a rest. Today had been such a crazy day that she needed to sit down and take it all in.

But first she had to get out of the teeny sundress. Brr.

🦇   🦇   🦇

Ivy had slipped out of the back door of the diner. She had to hide out behind a dumpster, while the hoards of cameramen snapped away at the six Mia wannabes and shouted questions at them: 'What can you tell us about Jackson?' and 'Which one of you is best at cooking?'

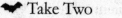

Olivia was at the opposite end to Charlotte, but Ivy smirked when she saw another candidate toss her hair right in Charlotte's face.

She didn't want anyone to catch on that there were two Olivias running around the set, but she didn't dare risk moving until the Mias had gone back inside and the paparazzi had dispersed.

She dodged behind a truck when two security guards walked past and then hid behind a stack of boxes when she saw a lighting technician. Ivy had to get out of Olivia's bunny clothes as soon as vampirically possible.

'Oof!' As she stepped out from behind the boxes, she ran smack into the broad back of a guy dressed all in black. 'Uh, sorry.'

He turned around and smiled. 'I'm not. It's the closest I've got to you in days.'

'Brendan!' she exclaimed.

He gathered her up in a hug. 'You look so cute with a tan.'

'Ha ha,' she replied. 'How did you get on set?'

'It turns out Jerome is almost as fond of the Breakfast Bun as my girlfriend is.'

Ivy smiled. 'Well, I'm desperate to change before our double act is discovered.'

He pointed across the parking lot to a dark trailer. 'I bet that's someplace no one will see you.'

'That's Jessica's trailer.' Ivy caught on quickly. 'Genius! Just wait here and I'll grab my clothes from the costume trailer. I won't be able to change there because there's bound to be some extras hanging around, looking for accessories to "borrow".' Ivy ran between trailers to the costume trailer and ducked her head in, grabbing her bag before anyone saw her. Then she raced back to Brendan, crouching low in order to avoid being spotted.

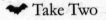

'Good rescue!' Brendan whispered.

They looked both ways. No one was coming, so they scurried across to Jessica's trailer.

'I'll be your watch dog,' Brendan said.

Ivy gave him a quick kiss on the cheek, yanked open the door and stepped inside. Jessica's trailer was dark and, even though it was twice as big as every other trailer on the lot, it was crammed with stuff. Jessica had clearly just stormed off and left everything behind.

There were bunches of flowers, now wilting from lack of water, and a bowl full of chocolate candies with all the colours picked out except the red ones.

'People actually demand that?' Ivy muttered.

She switched back into her normal clothes and then rummaged through the drawers of Jessica's vanity table to find some make-up remover. There were boxes of false eyelashes, bottles of hairspray and fake tan, and even some wart cream.

'Ew,' Ivy said.

She found some removal cream and wiped off as much of the tan as she could, until she felt almost herself again.

Just as she was about to leave, she heard Brendan outside coughing loudly.

Oh no, Ivy thought. *I've got nowhere to hide!*

She could see out of a side window and there were people milling around outside the trailer opposite. She knew that was Jackson's trailer; she could see him moving around inside, pausing by his dressing-table mirror.

Ivy watched as he leaned in close to the mirror.

What's he doing? Ivy wondered.

He was hunched over. His fingers were going to his eye. Ivy gasped as he popped out a contact lens with one finger. CONTACT LENS! Just like the one she put in every day to protect her vampire eyes from the sun.

Garlic clause or no, Ivy thought. *This is the evidence I've been waiting for! Jackson has to be a vampire.*

Chapter Ten

Ivy couldn't help feeling like she was tied to a stake while Olivia practically floated around her bedroom.

'It was sweet,' Olivia was saying. 'He was so nervous.'

'I know, but –' Ivy started.

'And the look on his face when I said yes!' Olivia interrupted.

'Yes, but –' Ivy tried again.

'And I couldn't stop smiling after.'

'Olivia!' Ivy said.

'What?' Olivia froze in place, holding on to

one of the bed posts.

'You know how you said you wanted a normal boyfriend?' Ivy began.

Olivia sat cross-legged on her bed and grinned at Ivy. 'I know, but he is normal. He's funny. He's cute. He can quote lines from Count Vira novels.'

Ivy sighed. 'But what if there is something you don't know about him?'

'There's tons I don't know about him,' Olivia said. 'And I hope I get to find out!'

Ivy had to tell her. 'I mean, what if he had a special relationship with his dentist?'

Olivia crinkled her nose. 'Do you mean he doesn't floss?'

'No.' She tried another track. 'I mean he wears contact lenses.'

Olivia looked confused. 'I don't care if he's near-sighted.'

There was no way to break it gently. 'Jackson

isn't near-sighted – I think he's a vampire.'

Olivia's jaw dropped open. 'What?'

Ivy went and sat next to her sister. 'The make-up artist has to order in tons of fake tan; Jackson has a no-garlic clause in his contract and I saw him taking out his contact lenses in his trailer. I'm sure of it. He's a night-walking, coffin-sleeping, sun-averse vampire.'

Ivy thought her sister's eyes looked a little watery.

It took a moment, but then Olivia seemed to gather herself. 'I know you can't tell who's a vampire and who's not, but I never would have thought . . . Well, I mean . . . Jackson? Really?' She sighed. 'That explains the burger.'

'I'm sorry. I had to tell you,' Ivy said.

Olivia nodded. 'He was just too perfect, I guess.' Olivia put her head on Ivy's shoulder. 'I think I could've gotten over the distance and the

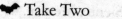

chaos, but this . . .' she trailed off and Ivy felt even worse. 'Being with a vampire is just not how I see my life playing out.' Olivia sniffled. 'It just makes everything way too complicated.'

'What are you going to do?' Ivy asked gently.

'I have to be honest with him. Tell him I know and call it off,' Olivia said.

'Are you *sure* you can't have a vampire boyfriend?' Ivy wondered if Olivia was making a choice she'd regret.

Olivia shook her head. 'I'm just lucky you discovered it now, before we'd had a first real date. I've only just found out about all this vampire stuff. A vampire boyfriend is just too much to handle right now.'

Olivia wrapped her arms around herself. Ivy had to give her a big hug. 'I'm really sorry,' she whispered. Ivy's first attempt at match-making had been a complete disaster.

'Me, too,' said Olivia. 'I guess I'll have to meet him somewhere we can talk without interruptions.' Olivia crinkled her nose. 'And I've got a good idea where that should be.'

🦇　　　🦇　　　🦇

'It's good to have you back,' Brendan said as he and Ivy walked down aisle nine at FoodMart, towards the secret entrance to the BloodMart. 'Air hockey isn't as much fun by myself.'

Ivy's black woolly beanie hat was pulled down over her ears and felt warm and cosy – no more sundresses in winter for her.

'It has been a crazy past few days,' Ivy admitted. Staying with Olivia was awesome but she was desperate for some real food. Her dad was coming back tonight, but she couldn't wait that long. Brendan had promised her a box of Count Cocoa Chew bars, as long as he could eat one right away. 'It's almost like the movie was an alien invasion.'

Brendan shook his head. 'Aliens wouldn't have lured you away from me with silver bangles and promises of fame and fortune.'

'Beetroot,' Ivy said, poking her tongue out at her boyfriend. They were at the STAFF ONLY door and that was the new password. George unlocked the door and they headed down the quiet, dark stairwell.

'I think my days as an extra are over,' Ivy said. 'Especially if Olivia gets the part. They wouldn't want her double hovering in the background.'

'When does she find out?' Brendan wanted to know.

'Sometime today,' Ivy said. 'Probably after her big conversation with Jackson.' Olivia's plan to call off their date was completely kooky, but Ivy didn't want to interfere any more in her sister's love life.

Ivy checked her watch – Olivia would be

meeting Jackson any moment now.

She pushed open the door and made straight for the candy aisle but stopped so suddenly that Brendan bumped into the back of her.

Browsing through the chocolate bars was a blonde bombshell wearing super-high heels and being fawned over by an entourage.

'It's . . . it's . . . Jessica Phelps!' Ivy stuttered, taking a step back and knocking into a display of Marshmallow Platelets that were on sale. 'What is she doing here?' Jessica had stormed off the movie set a few days ago and it wasn't like Franklin Grove was on the celebrity circuit.

'Beating us to the last of the Count Cocoa Chews?' Brendan said, with a longing glance down the candy aisle.

Jessica caught sight of Ivy staring and sighed. Then put on a huge fake smile. 'Hi, there! Do you want my autograph?'

Ivy was so confused. Why would Jessica be in the BloodMart?

Jessica's high heels clicked on the glossy floor as she came over, standing a little too close to Brendan for Ivy's liking. 'If you don't have a pen, don't worry!' She pulled a pen covered in rhinestones out of her big beige bag and scrawled her name across a box of Puffy Plasma Cookies. 'There you go!'

Ivy didn't even like Puffy Plasmas but she took the box so that she could ask, 'What brings you back to Franklin Grove? Didn't you quit the movie?'

Jessica tossed her hair, making Brendan duck to avoid getting whacked. 'There was a huge poll in *Celeb Weekly* and it turns out my fans would love to see J-Squared – that's me and Jackson – together on screen. Isn't that to die for? So I'm taking my part back. No more of that publicity stunt silliness trying to find some amateur.'

'Uh, yeah,' Ivy mumbled. 'Killer.'

Poor Olivia, Ivy thought. *That means even if Philippe picks her, she won't get the part.*

It took a second to register, but then Ivy realised: if Jessica was in the BloodMart, that meant . . . she was . . . a vampire!

Ivy's head started to spin. *Does that mean . . .?*

Fake tan wasn't entirely conclusive. And the J-02 could stand for Jessica, not Jackson. Ivy remembered the bowl of red candies in Jessica's trailer and the fake tan in the drawer.

Maybe Jackson really was near-sighted.

'Ivy, are you all right? You're turning pink,' Brendan put a hand on her shoulder.

'Uh, hey,' Ivy said to Jessica.

The movie star put one hand on her hip, and it was clear that Ivy had already worn out her welcome. 'Is J-Squared a match made

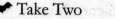

in the graveyard?'

'You mean, is Jackson a creature of the night?' Jessica laughed like Ivy had just suggested she take a supporting role. 'Of course not!'

'No. Of course not. Who would think such a thing?' Ivy mumbled. 'Thanks.'

She pulled Brendan into the cereal aisle.

'Should I take you home?' Brendan was looking worried, so Ivy had to explain.

'I've done a stupid, stupid thing.' She shook the autographed box of Plasma Puffs with every word. 'Jessica is the vampire, not Jackson,' she said. 'And that means Olivia doesn't have to break it off with him.' There could be a silver lining to this cloud of doom. 'I've got to tell her.' But then the image of Olivia waiting for Jackson flashed into her mind. 'Oh no.'

'You're turning pink again,' Brendan said.

Ivy knew that any moment now, Olivia was

going to make a big speech to Jackson about why they couldn't be together – because he was a vampire. But since he wasn't, it meant that Olivia was about to break the First Law of the Night! There were a tomb-load of reasons Ivy had to stop her.

'Come on,' Ivy said, shoving the Puffs in with the Marshmallow Platelets and charging full speed up the stairwell.

'But what about my Count Cocoa Chew?' Brendan called after her.

'If you help me get to Olivia, you can have all the Count Cocoa Chews you like!'

🦇　　　🦇　　　🦇

Olivia was perched on the edge of a low stone table in the oldest cemetery in Franklin Grove waiting for Jackson. Even though it was daylight, and Olivia knew that vampires didn't jump out of the shadows and bite people any more, she

225

didn't want to wait by herself for any longer than she had to.

She hoped Jackson would understand what she was trying to say by meeting here – she wanted him to understand that she wasn't freaked out by him being a vampire. It just meant things couldn't move forward between them.

A dark figure caught her eye, moving from one tree to the next on the other side of the graveyard.

The figure came nearer and Olivia could see that whoever it was was trying not to be seen.

She slipped off the table, darted behind a statue of an angel and crouched down. *Maybe this wasn't such a good idea*, she thought. Anyone could be wandering around this graveyard!

Then the person stepped out of the shadow. 'Harker Films' was written in big bold letters across his jacket. Jackson. He was in his security-guard disguise again.

He was looking right at the table where she'd been sitting. 'Olivia?' he called.

He must have seen her waiting there and now was wondering why she'd disappeared. 'Sorry I'm late. I thought I had some paparazzi following me, so I did a couple of extra loops.'

Olivia felt like a goof ball as she straightened up and stepped out from behind the statue. 'I, uh, was just doing a little weeding.'

Jackson smiled and came over. 'You'll have a tough time doing this whole place by hand.'

'Oh, no. I just, uh . . .' Olivia didn't want her nerves to take over. She didn't want to say anything stupid. And now that he was here, looking at her with his beautiful blue eyes, she didn't really want to break it off either. But it was for the best.

'I'm teasing,' Jackson said, taking off his hat

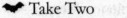

and looking around with a wry grin. 'This isn't exactly what I had in mind for our first date, but the place definitely has atmosphere.'

'I just wanted to show you that I wasn't scared,' Olivia said.

'OK,' Jackson replied, but she wasn't sure he completely understood her point. He leaned against the table next to her. 'Look, I've got something to tell you and I'm pretty sure you're not going to like it.'

Olivia's heart went out to him. He was biting his lip and looked pretty worried about what he was going to say. She wanted to spare him the stress. 'I already know.'

'You know?' Jackson look shocked.

If he hadn't read the *Vamp!* magazine article about Olivia and Ivy, then of course it would take him by surprise that a human could be in on the vampire secret. 'Yes, and it doesn't bother me.'

'I don't know how you know, but why doesn't it bother you? It would bother me,' Jackson replied.

'Don't say that,' Olivia said. She didn't want him to be unhappy about who he was. 'There's nothing wrong with being yourself.'

'Myself?' Jackson said. 'I don't have any control over it.'

'Of course not,' Olivia said, thinking of her and Ivy's history. 'You can't choose who you are.'

Jackson looked totally confused. 'Are we talking about the same thing?'

It must be hard for any vampire to expose the secret, after living their whole lives upholding the First Law. Olivia decided that if she just laid it all out and said the 'v' word herself, it would prove she knew and then she could tell Jackson what she brought him here to say.

She took one of his gloved hands in her mittens and took a deep breath.

'Jackson,' she said. 'Listen to me . . .'

Chapter Eleven

'Hello!' A familiar voice interrupted her. 'Yoo-hoo! Hi, guys!' Olivia saw Ivy trampling through the grass towards them, waving like crazy.

'Has she had too many sugary drinks?' Jackson asked.

'Good question,' Olivia replied cautiously.

'Hi!' Ivy called as she neared.

Brendan, bringing up the rear, looked as baffled as Olivia felt.

'Hey, Olivia,' Ivy said, totally out of breath and red-faced. 'Oh, hi, Jackson.'

'Hi,' Jackson replied, but he didn't take his eyes off Olivia.

Ivy plonked herself in between Olivia and Jackson. 'What are you guys up to?'

Olivia searched Ivy's a face for a sign. Why was her sister acting so super-cheerful? Ivy knew why she'd brought Jackson here but she was acting like it was the most normal thing in the world to hang out in a graveyard. *Which*, Olivia supposed, *for Ivy it is.*

'Just talking,' Olivia said, trying to put *Go away* into her voice.

'Jackson, this is Brendan,' Ivy said. 'Brendan, this is Jackson.' When the two guys were saying their hellos, Ivy knocked Olivia on the arm to get her attention and mouthed, 'NOT A VAMPIRE!'

Did Ivy just say what I think she just said?

Ivy made rabbit ears with her fingers and was making hopping motions when Jackson turned back. Ivy quickly dropped her hand.

Rabbit. Bunny. Suddenly Olivia realised what Ivy was trying to say. Jackson was NOT a vampire!

'What do you think of our cemetery, Jackson?' Ivy said.

Not a vampire, not a vampire! kept running through Olivia's mind. That meant that she didn't have to break it off with him. She wanted to bounce around among the graves with happiness, until she realised that it meant she'd brought him to the oddest place for their first date.

'It's very nice,' Jackson replied.

He must think I'm insane, Olivia thought.

'I just wanted us to have a quick look at some of the sights of the city,' Olivia said. 'But maybe now we should go somewhere warmer.'

The foursome walked down the stone path towards the street.

'What about the stuff we were talking about?' Jackson asked her quietly so Ivy and Brendan couldn't hear.

'Uh . . .' Olivia started. *If he isn't a vampire*, Olivia realised, *then he had something entirely different to tell me*. Olivia gulped. *And I'm not going to like it.*

Just then, a sleek silver Mercedes pulled up.

'Uh oh,' Jackson said. 'I've been discovered.'

The door opened and Amy Teller emerged. 'Jackson! I've been looking everywhere for you!'

'Hi, Amy,' he called and led everyone over to the sidewalk.

'What are you doing dressed as a security guard?' she demanded. 'Philippe wants you and Jessica to start filming this afternoon.'

Olivia was confused. 'Jessica?'

'That's what I was trying to tell you,' Jackson said. 'Philippe cancelled your auditions because Jessica came back to the movie.'

'Oh.' Olivia felt like a deflated balloon.

First, she'd dragged Jackson to a graveyard, almost blurted out the biggest secret ever and, finally, found out that she had lost her chance to be in a movie. *Not a good day*, Olivia thought.

'Look, I –' Jackson started, but Amy cut him off.

'We *really* need to get back,' Amy said.

'I'm really sorry,' Jackson said and stepped into the car. 'I hope I get to see you around, somewhere? Goodbye, Olivia.'

'Goodbye, Jackson,' Olivia whispered.

As he was shutting the door, Olivia heard Amy ask, 'What were you doing hanging out in a graveyard?'

🦇　　　🦇　　　🦇

The car sped off towards the movie set. Ivy followed a dazed Olivia as she wandered down the sidewalk and sat on a wooden bench.

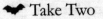

Ivy put her arm around her sister. 'Aw, sis, I'm sorry.'

Olivia hugged her back and wiped away her tears. 'Not your fault. Jackson and I just weren't meant to be.'

'At least you didn't blow the coffin lid off our vamp secret,' Ivy said, trying to point out the positive.

'It was pretty close,' Olivia admitted.

'How about getting something to eat?' Brendan suggested hopefully.

'Since the Meat & Greet is currently J-Squared central – that's Jackson and Jessica central apparently,' Ivy explained to a bewildered Olivia, 'let's hit the Juice Bar.'

'Woohoo!' Brendan said.

That night, Ivy was sipping hot chocolate with Olivia next to her on the Abbott's couch.

Her dad was back from his trip and she wanted to hear all about it, mostly to distract herself from all the guilt she was feeling over Jackson and Olivia.

Mr Vega said he had come straight from the airport to thank Mrs Abbott for looking after Ivy and to pick her up. Of course, Mrs Abbott had laid out a vegetarian feast, which he was picking at to be polite.

'Enough of those boring details,' said Mr Vega, 'I understand it has been an eventful few days, in my absence. Anyone going to fill me in on the latest news?'

When Olivia finished explaining that the original movie's star had returned, Mr Vega said, 'Oh, I'm sorry to hear that. I think you would make a fine actress, Olivia.'

Ivy saw her sister smile again. *Maybe she's going to be OK*, Ivy thought.

'It's probably better that a real actress is doing it,' Olivia replied. 'But I've decided to try out for the next school play.'

'Unless Charlotte's going for the part, then you might *really* break a leg! Hers!' Ivy joked.

As Olivia chuckled, someone rang the front doorbell. Mrs Abbott stood up to get it and Ivy peeked out the window to see who it was. A flash of blonde hair, and she knew right away.

Olivia hurried down the hallway, squeezed past her mom and opened the door.

'Hi, Jackson,' she said, although about a thousand other things were running through her head to say like, *Graveyards aren't that bad*, or *How about a smoothie?* or *I'm not as crazy as I seem, honestly*.

'Hey,' he replied, his smile making Olivia's heart go squidgy like a gummy bear.

He was wearing his brown cowboy boots again, faded jeans and a blue long-sleeved T-shirt that matched his eyes. A dark car was waiting for him by her mailbox and she could see a chauffeur inside.

'I didn't get to say everything I wanted to say today at the graveyard,' he said, and she could see his breath in the cold air.

Olivia stepped outside on to the porch and pulled the door closed behind her. She was guessing that she didn't want her whole family to hear this.

'I wanted to say that before Jessica came back, Philippe had decided to choose you.'

Olivia let out a squeal. 'Really?'

Jackson laughed. 'Really.'

Even though it would never happen now, it was super-exciting to know that a Hollywood director thought she had the potential to be a movie star.

'And since Philippe has decided that he "discovered" you–' Jackson put on a silly French accent when he said 'discovered' – 'he's ordered the writers to create a new part.'

Olivia couldn't believe it.

'Since Chase only sees Mia in his imagination until the last Franklin Grove, Philippe decided that he's going to make this Franklin Grove the second to last one, and Chase is going to be tempted to stay by another girl . . . you.'

'Me?' Olivia squeaked.

Jackson moved forward when he replied, 'That won't be too hard for me to act.'

Olivia held her breath. *Did he just say that?* she thought.

'It's only a small part, but I know you'll be great in it.' Jackson held up a folder full of papers. 'I've brought some forms that your parents have to read and sign, if they're happy for you to do it.'

Olivia took the papers. 'Thank you so much. I know that none of this would have happened if it weren't for you.'

'You're welcome,' Jackson replied. 'But you're the one who did it.'

Just then, Olivia heard a clunk against the window and saw the curtain inside being closed hurriedly.

'I think I better ask you to come in,' Olivia said, realising for the first time that she wasn't even wearing a coat.

'I'd love that.' Jackson smiled and she realised why she didn't need one.

'Oh, there's just one last thing,' Jackson said. 'The new character is a goth, so you might want to get some tips from that twin of yours.' He winked.

Olivia grinned. 'Took you long enough.'

🦇   🦇   🦇

Ivy was only a little embarrassed about being caught watching Olivia and Jackson. When they walked into the living room together, they looked so right together that she wished she'd never tried to keep them apart.

Olivia looked like she was going to burst with some news.

'I got a part in the movie!' she announced.

'Yay!' Ivy cheered. Mrs Abbott clapped and Mr Vega looked like he knew it was going to happen all along.

As Jackson introduced himself and explained to her parents about Olivia's part and that she would only miss two days of school, Ivy went over to Olivia and whispered, 'Did he ask you out again?'

'No, it was all very professional.'

'Not all of it,' Ivy hissed back. 'I saw the way he was looking at you!'

'Can I get you a drink, Jackson?' Mrs Abbott said.

'No, thank you, but do any of those delicious-looking snacks have meat in them?' he replied.

'We're vegetarians,' Mrs Abbott explained.

'Excellent!' Jackson said. 'Me too.'

Ivy smacked her hand to her forehead. Typical. Only she would mistake a vegetarian for a vampire.

'But what about that burger that Curtis gave you?' Olivia asked. 'I believe the exact words were "hunk of cow"?'

Jackson had his hands full with crackers dipped in hummus. 'Oh, he was just teasing. That burger is the best garden burger on the circuit – and Curtis keeps that oven just for us veggies to make sure there's no contamination.'

Olivia let out a little sigh.

They really are perfect for each other, Ivy thought.

Jackson cleared his throat. 'There is one other

thing I would like to ask your permission for; something that isn't on the forms.'

Ivy and Olivia watched as their parents looked at Jackson.

'I would like to take Olivia to the movies tomorrow night.'

Olivia grabbed Ivy's hand, and Ivy smiled. Jackson had already won over Mr Vega just by asking, and Mr Abbott stood up to shake Jackson's hand. Mrs Abbott let out an Olivia-like squeal and went to get her camera.

'That is, if you'll go with me?' Jackson said to Olivia. 'It's your decision, after all.'

'Of course I will,' she said.

Ivy plonked down on the carpet next to her dad's chair, happy that everything had worked out. There was nothing better in the world than seeing her sister happy. Nothing could spoil things now. She nudged over a little, to avoid the airline sticker on his bag that was poking against her neck.

She pushed it away and read the letters LAX. *That's not Dallas*, Ivy thought. *That's Los Angeles.*

Ivy watched everyone follow each other into the kitchen for some lemonade, but stayed sitting on the couch alone. *Is Dad telling us the whole truth . . .?* Ivy wondered. *Why would he lie?*

Her phone beeped with a text message from Brendan: 'Everything all right now?'

Ivy texted back, 'I'm not sure . . .'

Could there be another secret to unravel?

Find out in the sixth book, coming soon:

The twins are in Transylvania, to meet their vampire family. Olivia is nervous – there's a lot at stake. But a smooth-talking boy is immediately taken with her. Ivy can't believe it – it's nearly Valentine's Day and her twin is spending time with a vampire prince!

Sink your teeth into this!

Being a new girl sucks. But then Olivia Abbot meets her long-lost twin sister, Ivy. They're as different as day and night – and Ivy has a grave secret. But it won't stop them getting to know each other's worlds. After all, blood is thicker than water – and it's certainly tastier!

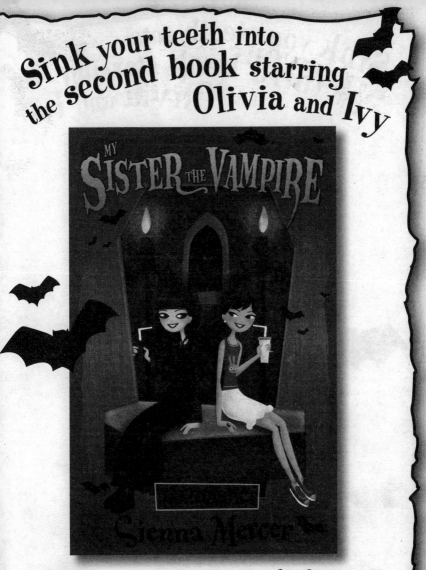

MY
SISTER THE VAMPIRE

Sienna Mercer

Sink your teeth into the third book starring Olivia and Ivy

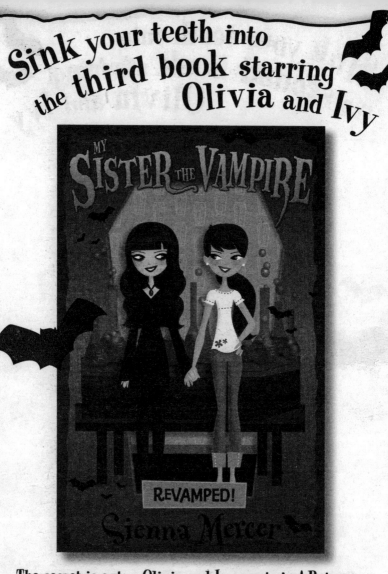

The secret is out – Olivia and Ivy are twins! But some people are turning in their coffins about it. Ivy's adoptive dad doesn't believe Olivia won't betray the Franklin Grove vampires. To prove she can be trusted, Olivia must pass three tests – but not just any old tests. These are challenges to really get the blood pumping!

Sink your teeth into the fourth book starring Olivia and Ivy

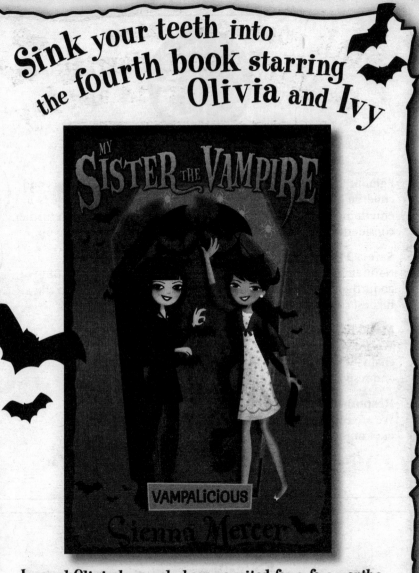

MY
SISTER THE VAMPIRE

VAMPALICIOUS

Sienna Mercer

Ivy and Olivia have only been reunited for a few months and already they can't imagine life without each other. But Ivy's dad is moving to Europe – taking Ivy with him! Olivia and Ivy need to change his mind, but will the skills of two crafty twins be enough to stop a vampire from spreading his wings?

EGMONT PRESS: ETHICAL PUBLISHING

Egmont Press is about turning writers into successful authors and children into passionate readers – producing books that enrich and entertain. As a responsible children's publisher, we go even further, considering the world in which our consumers are growing up.

Safety First
Naturally, all of our books meet legal safety requirements. But we go further than this; every book with play value is tested to the highest standards – if it fails, it's back to the drawing-board.

Made Fairly
We are working to ensure that the workers involved in our supply chain – the people that make our books – are treated with fairness and respect.

Responsible Forestry
We are committed to ensuring all our papers come from environmentally and socially responsible forest sources.

**For more information, please visit our website at
www.egmont.co.uk/ethical**

Mixed Sources
Product group from well-managed forests and other controlled sources
www.fsc.org Cert no. TT-COC-002332
© 1996 Forest Stewardship Council

Egmont is passionate about helping to preserve the world's remaining ancient forests. We only use paper from legal and sustainable forest sources, so we know where every single tree comes from that goes into every paper that makes up every book.

This book is made from paper certified by the Forestry Stewardship Council (FSC), an organisation dedicated to promoting responsible management of forest resources. For more information on the FSC, please visit **www.fsc.org**. To learn more about Egmont's sustainable paper policy, please visit **www.egmont.co.uk/ethical**.